THE NUCLEAR PULSE THREAT

RICHARD SLOANE

ISBN: 978-1-957956-49-7 (sc)
ISBN: 978-1-957956-51-0 (hc)
ISBN: 978-1-957956-50-3 (e)

Rev. date: 09/22/2022

ACKNOWLEDGEMENTS

First, I would like to thank from the bottom of my heart the entire editorial staff at Leavitt Peak Press for making the book look so good, especially Sam Davis and Mia Baker who oversaw the entire process so professionally.

I would also like to thank very much my good friend Michael Black for doing an initial edit of my manuscript and spotting a large number of idiocies which I otherwise would probably have missed.

NB This manuscript is protected under the Official Secrets Act and anyone under an Alpha plus security clearance found to have opened it will be punishable by the full force of the law under the provisions of the said Act.

CONTENTS

CHAPTER 1

WEDNESDAY PM

I was working in my office as usual on a cool and rainy afternoon in late July trying to read the millions of files which seem to pile up on my desk indiscriminately every second of my working day. I knew of course that they were all important and deserving of my attention (I was after all responsible for the safety and security of the realm) but I wondered what crimes I had committed in a past life to tie me down to a desk as I was. What I really wanted was to go out on the streets and get my hands dirty. Every time I turned around there seemed to be another terrorist threat to deal with or something equally horrible but they were all small beer really, the odd fanatic and suicide bomber who all had to be monitored and deterred in one way or another, although it wasn't of course small beer for the victims for whom the effects could be devastating. If the public knew how many threats were thwarted by my people, they would probably be totally horrified. But I wanted something substantial to get my teeth into, something more serious than the usual run-of-the-mill suspects. And if this sounds callous, then I apologise but I was itching for some proper action. I knew I really wasn't cut out to be a desk jockey. However my prayers were about to be answered – and how!

I got a call out of the blue, put through by my secretary, from Peter, the secretary of the COBRA committee (*the committee which is called in the face of a national emergency*), asking me to come immediately to an extraordinary meeting which was being convened in its usual secure location under Whitehall. This was not a request, but more of an order, and, slinging my jacket on and checking that I had my all-important card on me which would get me into any facility in the country, I rushed out of the office and down to the car park. There I met Bill, our garage attendant, and asked him what the traffic was like across the bridge. He told me that it wasn't looking too good and asked me where I was going. 'Whitehall,' I replied. 'Probably best to take a taxi then,' he said, adding, 'Do you want me to get you one?' 'Yes, please,' I said, knowing that he had easy access to every taxi operator in the city, 'I am in a bit of a hurry.' He went into his little booth, made a quick phone call and was back inside 20 seconds. 'There'll be one waiting outside the main door within a minute,' he said. I thanked him and rushed up the one flight of stairs, not bothering to wait for the lift, and ran outside just as an empty taxi drew up. I jumped in and said 'Whitehall and step on it, please,' I said and we screamed off, the tyres burning rubber.

All the while I'd been thinking hard about what the

flap could possibly be about. We'd had no reports of any immediate security threats, the only reason I could think of why *I'd* been summoned so abruptly. There is, in fact, only one COBRA committee although different experts are called in depending on the type of threat. So, for example, the SAGE committee, consisting mainly of medical experts, were brought in to advise during the COVID pandemic a few years ago, but Peter knew who I was and what my job entailed and I could only assume it was something to do with internal security.

Perhaps now might be a good time to introduce myself a little more formally. My name is Jack Sanderson and my official job title is Director of Operations for MI5 (*the rough equivalent of the FBI in the States*). I was responsible to only two people, the Prime Minister and my ultimate boss, Sir Maurice, the Director General, a wily old bird who was now in his mid-seventies but still as sharp as a tack. He'd been my mentor way back when I first came out of the army and joined MI5 and he'd been the one to promote me up to my present lofty status. I was also a long-standing member of the COBRA committee which usually only met at times agreed at least several days before. So the present situation was, if not unprecedented, at least unusual enough to pique my interest. Ok, enough about me.

When I arrived a few minutes later at my destination, having paid off the driver and given him a substantial tip for his speed, I at once ran down the grand marble staircase in the Foreign Office and along the long, underground corridor to a big steel door guarded by a couple of burly, heavily-armed Military Policemen, one of whom asked politely if I was expected. I said, 'Yes,' and presented him with my card. He scrutinised it carefully, checking my photo, and then, inserting it into an optical scanner, scanned my irises and finally my fingerprints, all of which information was on my card. I knew this procedure would be done with everybody who entered the labyrinth beyond right up the PM himself and I didn't resent it as I had been instrumental in having it set up. But soon it was all done and then I was through the door and running down another long corridor. I came to a T junction where I knew if I turned left, it would take me straight underground to a small room directly under 10 Downing St and from there up in a guarded lift to the PM's residence itself. However, I turned right, passing a few closed doors on my way, and soon reached my destination, another closed door, also guarded, with just an anonymous number on it. The guard checked my card again and ticked my name off on a list in front of him and waved me through.

CHAPTER 2

A LITTLE LATER THE SAME AFTERNOON

I was now in the Holy of Holies, one of the most secure rooms in the country, and I glanced around the big table to see who I recognised. At once I spotted the General who had recently been appointed Chief of the General Staff, the top position in the British army, and wondered what he was doing here, my interest going up another notch. Most of the others I knew personally and I waved to them and plonked myself down on an available chair. Then, however, I noticed Toby come through the door, my counterpart in MI6 and a chap I had worked closely with before and one whom I liked a lot and, more to the point, trusted. He saw me and came over, sitting in the empty chair next to me. 'What's going on, old chap?' he whispered. 'No idea, mate,' I whispered back. So we just had to sit there for whatever transpired.

We only had to wait a short time before the PM bumbled in followed by his private secretary, looking as dishevelled as ever but underneath his unkempt exterior

I knew a smart political brain was ticking over. He got down to business at once turning to Peter and saying, 'Do we have a quorum?' 'Yes,' came the immediate reply. 'Good. Thank you all for coming in at such short notice. I'd like to pass you straight over to Geoffrey, my PPS.'

His private secretary stood up and went to the back of the room where he inserted a memory stick into a screen reader and switched everything on, turning down the lights as he did so. A neatly-typed letter came up which said:

"Dear PM,

I hope you know what an EMP weapon can do to your electricity grid. Just to remind you, it will mimic the effect of a vast solar sun flare. We have acquired two medium-range nuclear-armed missiles, one aimed directly above London, the other above Washington which we are prepared to detonate high enough in the atmosphere to do irreparable damage to your grid. We guarantee they will be detonated unless:

1. You take immediate steps to release **all** ISIS and Al-Qaeda prisoners whom you have detained illegally in detention camps and prisons all over the world.
2. You pay us a sum of $500 million as reparation for detaining these prisoners to be paid into a numbered account, whose details we will send you shortly.

You have a **maximum** of two weeks to begin to do these two things. If we see no concrete progress on both these things, the warheads will be released. We know that both things are doable.

One other thing: Please do not try to find our base of operations. If we catch even a whisper of your coming after us (and we can assure you we will), the warheads will be released at once.

A similar letter to this one has been sent to the President of the USA.

If you value your way of life, we suggest you take this very seriously.

Yours very sincerely,
ISIS / Al-Qaeda"

There were gasps of shock around the room as we all assimilated the letter. Then Geoffrey said, 'This came through at 2pm today in the normal post. It was postmarked 'Brixton' and, according to our forensics people, there were no fingerprints on it or on the envelope itself except for the normal ones you would expect, the post person and the people in my office whose job it is to scan all the mail. Now I'll pass you back to the PM.'

'Thanks, Geoffrey. Now the first thing I need to know is, could this be some sort of sick hoax? Needless to say, I've already been on the phone to the US president and he has indeed received a similar letter. However, his advisors are asking him not to treat it seriously. They say their security community has intercepted no radio traffic suggesting that such an attack could be imminent. That said, however, they do admit that ISIS has quite recently changed their codes yet again and the NSA (*the main American government intelligence gathering facility, equivalent to the British GCHQ*) hasn't managed to break the new ones. I need your ideas urgently, ladies and gentlemen.'

There was silence in the room for a few seconds and then the Chief of the Defence Staff spoke up. 'We have been worried about such an attack for about 15 years now and what it says in the letter about the total destruction of our electricity grid if a nuclear device is set off high enough in the atmosphere is unfortunately true. We have done a number of simulations based on this premise over the past few years and to say that its effects would be catastrophic would be an understatement. It would probably take us years to recover. Can we afford not to take it seriously?'

'Thank you, David. What do you think about it, Jack? You have dealt with maniacs like these before if I remember rightly.'

This was my cue to speak. 'Yes, sir, I have indeed. Several things spring to mind immediately. The first is that, like the Americans, we have not heard a whisper about such an operation being in the offing. But this is no indication that one might not be.' I was thinking back to the events I described in a former memoir which I called *The Dirty Bomb Affair,* when we only caught the bombers at the last second due to the breaking of their codes by the NSA. 'And the second is that it's signed jointly by ISIS and Al-Qaeda. This could be a very worrying development if it's not a hoax. If they have indeed joined forces, even if only for this one operation, it goes against everything we know about the two organisations which have had multiple disagreements in the past. But I'm with the General on this one and would argue that we can't afford not take it seriously.'

'I'm inclined to agree with you. Anybody got anything else to add?' But there was silence around the table. 'OK. Where do we go from here?'

'The first thing,' I said, 'is that we're going to have to keep the whole investigation totally secret. If there is even a whiff of a nuclear weapon being directed against the country, the public will panic for sure and everything might end up even worse than our electricity grid going off-line for however long it will take to fix.'

'Hear! Hear!' resounded from around the table.

'Good point,' the PM said now, making a note on a piece of paper.

The briefing I'd been given on an EMP threat was coming back to me now and I asked the General what the range of a medium-range nuclear weapon was.

'Anywhere between 1,000 and about 3,000 kilometres,' he replied.

'And does anyone know how far it is from London to Washington in a straight line?'

Peter got busy on the computer and came up with an answer very quickly. '3,669 miles or about 5,900 kilometres,' he said.

'Ok. So if we assume the worst, it would theoretically

be possible for a ship in Mid-Atlantic to hit both targets. The reason I asked was because I remember now being told that the simplest way for a terrorist to cause an EMP explosion would be to put the missile on a ship.'

'Yes,' Toby said now. 'I remember that too. We were told that the weapon would probably either be launched from a ship or a satellite or even, if I remember rightly, from a balloon. And given that ISIS or Al-Qaeda don't have satellite capabilities yet, as far as we know, and a balloon attack is ridiculous, a ship would certainly seem to be the likeliest possibility.'

I was glad to get Toby's support and glanced at him gratefully but continued, 'If that is the case, it should be possible to find the vessel and neutralise it before they can release the weapons. Has anyone heard about a hi-jacking in the Atlantic recently?.... No, neither have we. So I think we can assume that if this threat is real, ISIS or Al-Qaeda have chartered or more likely bought their own ship. But we'll certainly have to tread very carefully.'

'Thank you very much for that, Jack,' the PM said now. 'I concur with what's been said and propose to put Jack in overall charge of the operation as it affects our domestic security directly and also because he's had more experience of these bastards than anyone else here. He's the most likely to be able to predict what might happen on the ground. So I expect everyone to give him all and any help he needs. Is that clear? And I want total secrecy on this. If anyone leaks anything at all, I'll have their balls on a plate.'

I winced at his colourful language but said 'Thank you for your trust in me, PM,' wondering if I'd just been given a poisoned chalice.

'I'll now need to brief the President on what we've decided,' he said, picking up his papers and sweeping out. The meeting broke up now, everyone going their separate ways. Toby followed me out saying wryly, 'Rather you than me, mate.' But I was too busy thinking about priorities to respond to this and just said 'I guess you'll be going back now to report to your boss,' to which his response was, 'As I guess you'll be doing to yours. Well, you know where to find me,' he concluded before we parted company.

CHAPTER 3

LATER ON THE SAME DAY

Toby was quite right, of course. The first thing I did when I got back to the office was to brief Sir M on the meeting. His comment on the letter, which I had copied down in my own version of shorthand, was terse and to the point. 'Well, I suppose it was inevitable. It was just a question of time.' Then he added, 'I suppose it'll be all hands to the pumps now?'

'Yes, indeed,' I replied. 'Could you possibly deal with all my routine bumf for a while, Sir, until this thing is resolved one way or another?'

'As you've been tasked by the PM to do whatever's necessary to sort out this problem, the answer of course is yes.'

'Thank you very much, Sir,' I said gratefully. 'I'll get my secretary to bring up the files.' And with those words I left him looking more serious than I'd seen him for some time.

The next priority was to assemble my inner circle that I trusted to the hilt and beyond. To this end, I called my deputy, Alan, and, giving him a list of their names, asked him how many of them were in the building. 'All except two who are on annual leave, Mike Beavis and Susannah Esteban,' he replied promptly.

'Ok,' I said, 'we'll have to do without them. Now can you book a secure conference room and get everybody together in about half an hour?'

'Yes, sure, sir. What's going on?'

'All will be revealed in the fullness of time,' I told him and he had to be content with that. Next I knew I had to ring my wife, Pamela, and warn her that I'd almost certainly be late back this evening. She was out running but answered her mobile at once and said, 'OK, darling. Shall I wait up for you tonight?' 'Probably not worth it,' I told her. She knew how occasionally in times of emergency I had to stay very late at the office. 'Ok,' she said, 'I'll leave something in the fridge for you.'

'Thanks, darling. See you when I do. Got to rush now.' And I hung up, thinking now of the list of things I wanted to say to my team as I started scribbling furiously in my notebook. The half hour was soon up and I left my office, telling my secretary, Sarah, to pass all my files to the Director General. She was used to my infrequent emergencies and knew she'd be put in the loop when I was ready to tell her, hardly blinking an eye. 'Big flap on, is there, sir?' she said as I disappeared. 'You could say that,' I replied.

I went into the conference room which Alan had booked for us and found everybody waiting and wondering what was going on. There were eight people in the room in total, enough I hoped – for now at least. 'Thanks for coming at such short notice,' I said, realising at once that I was echoing the words of the PM at the afternoon meeting. 'This will be our base of operations from now on and the door must be securely locked at all times to everybody, including the cleaners. Is that clear?'

'Yes, sir!' they all chorused.

I continued by giving them almost exactly the same briefing, if slightly truncated, as I'd given Sir M of the COBRA meeting, reading the letter from my notes as I had with him. There were gasps of horror as I went through it slowly, just as there had been earlier in the afternoon. I continued by saying, 'I don't need to tell you how serious a threat this is to the entire country. An electro-magnetic pulse threat is something the armed forces have simulated several times and they all agree that it poses as serious a threat as a full-blown nuclear attack. They themselves would be operating almost completely blind as all their computers would probably be paralysed as will everything else in the country which operates on electricity. We'd be back in the Stone Age. The fact that the USA is not taking the threat seriously is, to my mind, almost completely irresponsible but let's leaves them out of the equation for the moment. As I'm sure you're aware, they are rather over-reliant on their supposed superiority in technology. Now, what can we do about it? If I'm right about these wretched bombs being on a ship, I think it should be easy enough to locate. But first we need the largest scale map you can find of the North Atlantic showing both London and Washington. I'm sure Toby will be doing the same but I'd like to check we're singing from the same hymn sheet. Oh, I'm sorry. I forgot to tell you he was at the meeting too. Alan, can you go down to the map room and see what you can come up with and be back here ASAP. Meanwhile I'll be handing out other assignments.'

'Sure thing, boss,' he said as he disappeared.

'Now, what about the rest of you? It seems to me that it's important to try to find out where the money came from for an operation of this size and also where it was planned and who planned it. If, God forbid, it was planned here, I need most of you to go out on the streets to interview every one of your snitches, especially those with ties to ISIS or Al-Qaeda, and to ask them if they've heard anything at all about a large operation aimed at the UK and America. But keep your questions very general. No mention of nuclear weapons, OK? As for the money, I'd like Gloria and Ben to handle that end of things.' I knew that Gloria was one of the best hackers in the country, perfectly capable of getting into more or less any bank in the world and Ben was a worthy assistant. If my suspicions were right, we'd really need her to confirm or deny if the whole operation was state-sponsored or not. If, for example Russia or North Korea or Iran were giving it their support, then my political masters would need to be informed promptly. 'Now, where's that ruddy map?' And there I paused....

And right on cue, Alan returned, panting slightly and carrying a couple of large maps, one of which was a Mercator, showing the ocean slightly bent as if one was looking at a globe. 'Good man,' I said. 'Put the Mercator map up on the board.' And he did so. 'Now can somebody draw a straight line between Washington and London?' And Ben got up now, producing a pencil and a ruler from his pockets, and did exactly that. 'Thank you, Ben. Now can you find exactly the halfway point?' And he did that too, having measured the length of the line. 'Now can you draw a circle around it of approximately 100 kilometres in any direction?' This took him longer as he needed to refer to the map's scale to get it accurate but it was still quickly done. 'Now I need you to read me the coordinates of the circle.'

'I can't do that very accurately, I'm afraid, sir. I can only do it roughly as a square.'

'That's OK. Just do it, please.' And he did it, while everyone else looked on wonderingly, and I wrote them down in my notebook. 'Thanks, Ben. Now I need to get in touch with whoever's in charge of overseeing satellite surveillance in this part of the world and get them to do a comprehensive search of the area to see if there are any ships either stationary or moving around in a slow circle in it.' The team all got where I was coming from now and I heard a loud exhalation of breath. I looked at the tiny square on the map, lost in the vastness of the ocean, and wondered how long it would take to search it. What was it, about 10,000 square kilometres? Not too long I guessed but we didn't have long. This had to be done pronto. 'OK, everybody. This is *my* priority. Now, get out and start making lists of who you want to speak to but remember. Be very discreet! Regardless of whether you hear anything or not, I'll have other tasks for you tomorrow. I'll see everyone back here at 8 am tomorrow morning. Please refer to Alan for your assignments. I'd hate for you all to be tripping over one another's feet. It looks like none of us will be getting much sleep over the next two weeks unless America's predilection for burying one's head in the sand turns out to be justified. And don't forget, people: this all stays tip-top secret. No blabbing to anyone about it, not even within this building. Alan, stay behind, please.' And with those final words they all filed out, looking scared and not a little pensive.

When Alan and I were alone, I told him what I had asked them all to do during his short absence from the room and he nodded his approval. Then I said, 'I'll need you to be my backstop here if I have to leave the office at any point,' and he nodded again. 'Remember I'll always be available on my mobile.'

'At least until the bomb goes off,' he said mordantly and it was now my turn to nod.

'Exactly,' I said and there we left it and returned to our own offices.

CHAPTER 4

THE REST OF THAT DAY

I at once called Sir M and told him what I needed, a name, basically. He said, 'Leave it with me, old chap. I'll get back to you soonest.'

'Thank you, Sir,' I said and hung up. I spent the next half hour or so making another list of what I needed to tell my team the next morning, and then suddenly remembered another thing I had to do. I rang the PM's private office and asked to speak to his PPS. He came on the line almost immediately and I asked whether they'd received another communication from the terrorists regarding a bank account number they were supposed to put the 500 million into. He said 'Yes, we have indeed, Jack.' 'Can you give me the number and the name of the bank, please?' 'Hang on a minute.' He came back to me very quickly and gave me the number and name without asking why I needed them. I thanked him and rang off, immediately ringing Gloria and giving her the two items, knowing she'd know to prioritise them.

Then I remembered about Toby and called him on his mobile. 'Have you checked out possible co-ordinates yet for our ship?' I asked without preamble. 'Thought you'd never ask,' he said humorously. 'Yes, we did that just a few minutes ago. They came out as.... and he rattled them off.' I checked them against the ones Ben had given me and they tallied very closely. I told him this, then said, 'Thanks very much, Toby. That's a relief. It's good to have some corroboration of the position of our putative ship.'

'Anything we can do to help, old chap,' and, before he hung up, I told him about how I was about to ring somebody about re-positioning a satellite to try to find the bloody ship. 'Good luck with that,' he said and disconnected. I knew he'd be pursuing his own lines of investigation, mainly abroad, and I didn't want to ask him for any more help at the moment.

Sir M got back to me not long after and said, 'Ok, Jack. I have the name you wanted. It's Sir Philip Larkin, like the poet, and he's waiting for you to call him. His number is **********. He's the Commander of all our satellite surveillance equipment.'

'Thank you, Sir,' I said and promptly hung up and dialled the number he'd given me. I heard the phone ring at the other end and then it was picked up. 'Sir Philip Larkin's office,' a voice said.

'Can I speak to Sir Philip? My name's Jack Sanderson and I'm the Director of Operations at MI5.'

'Oh, yes, sir. We've been told you were going to ring. I'm putting you through now.' Then I heard a deep, posh voice say. 'Philip Larkin here. What can I do for you, Mr Sanderson? I must admit I was quite surprised when I got a call from the PM himself saying to give you any and every support.'

So I outlined the problem to him, giving him the coordinates, without going into specifics or mentioning nuclear warheads and he hummed and hawed a bit, then said: 'I don't think you quite realise the difficulty of repositioning satellites. You are asking for one with a high definition camera and videoing abilities. We don't have many of these and they are all positioned over Eastern Europe and the Far East at the moment. It will probably take at least a couple of days to get one in position.'

'We have very little time, Sir Philip. Could you possibly do it within 24 hours? It is a national emergency, I promise you.'

There was a long pause. 'I may be able to borrow one from the Americans. I can but ask.'

I thought about this for a second and then realised how useful it might be to get the USA on board as quickly as possible. 'Yes, by all means do that if you have to. Thanks very much, Sir Philip. Remember time is of the essence.'

'It always is, isn't it?' he said wryly.

'Let me give you my mobile number. You can ring me on it any time, day or night, as soon as you have any news for me.' And I gave him it. I heard him writing it down and we exchanged a couple of pleasantries before hanging up. Then I looked at my watch and was astonished to see it was 6.45 already. There really wasn't anything to keep me in the office any longer and I decided to go home to the loving arms of my wife and try to get a good night's sleep. After all I was in my mid-fifties now and knew I always operated better after a decent sleep. I'd leave all the routine work to the youngsters who I knew could get by on less. So I rang Alan and told him briefly the progress I'd made and where I was going, and then Sir M telling him also and thanking him again for dealing with all my routine work. He harrumphed and said, 'You'll owe me a large one when this is all over,' which made me laugh. There was now just one more call to make to Pamela to tell her what time I should be arriving and she squealed with delight before hanging up. On the way home I decided to write up my notes on the operation when I had the time as I had done five times already. *(Please see my other memoirs for details of these.)* It seemed to be meriting it.

When I got back, Pamela immediately asked, 'So, a big flap on, is there?' as I knew she would. She's always been curious about my job and what it entails. But I just replied, 'It could turn out that way,' and refused to answer any more questions. We had a lovely home-cooked dinner and then I just crashed out, exhausted by the events of the day, and was left undisturbed by phone calls the whole night through.

CHAPTER 5

THURSDAY AM

I got up early the next morning, had a quick shower and shave and an even quicker breakfast. Then I went down in the lift to our block's private garage and drove the few miles back to the office. It was still before the main rush hour of the day started so there wasn't much traffic, which gave me the opportunity to review what I needed to do. Once there I checked to find out if any of my team was in yet (it was still only 7.00) but none of them were. Probably all still sleeping – but I didn't begrudge them that. Even *they* needed their beauty sleep. I was just grateful to have such a good team. But now I started doing what I had really come into the office early for, making extensive notes on the case so far, trying not to forget any of the important details. It always helped me to see things written down – even in my awful scribble. It clarified my thoughts and was often useful in remembering things I needed or had forgotten to do. I knew, if my gut feeling was correct and this situation was going to spin out of control, I'd need to type them all up later and do lots of editing but I didn't mind that.

I was making good progress when I glanced at my watch and saw it was just coming up to 8.00. Time to stop and make my way to the meeting.

Back in the conference room, I looked around to make sure we were all present and correct and was pleased to see that indeed we were, even if several of them were yawning their heads off. I started by giving them a rundown of what I'd achieved the night before but ended by stressing the possible delay in repositioning a satellite. They all looked a bit gloomy at this but I said, 'All is not lost. Even if it takes a couple of days, we've still got time to control the situation,' and there were nods from around the table. 'Now, has anyone got anything at all to tell me?' And I looked around but several of them shook their heads sorrowfully. But then Lucy, one of the youngest on the team, spoke up.

'I did hear something but it might not be relevant. One of my snitches mentioned that, quite recently, ISIS seemed to be in the market for recruiting people with experience in operating submersibles. However, he stressed it was just a rumour and didn't put much store by it but, since the deep ocean seems to be of particular interest to you, sir, I thought I'd better mention it.'

'That could be an important part of the jigsaw, Lucy. Thanks a lot. Well done! Operating submersibles, eh? I feel sure there's a connection there somewhere but for the life of me I can't see what that's got to do with our putative nuclear problem. After all, the warheads have to be detonated in the high atmosphere to create a pulse effect. Unless the whole pulse scenario is a cover for something else? Oh well, I'm sure that little puzzle will be solved sooner rather than later. Anybody else?' And now Gloria spoke up. 'Yes, Gloria?'

'That bank account number and the bank it's associated with, which you gave us yesterday, were interesting. Ben and I have been running around in circles most of the night trying to verify whether they've got anything to do with ISIS or Al-Qaeda. The account certainly exists but the level of encryption associated with it is unprecedented in my experience, which has got to be suspicious, doesn't it? However, that said, we are making progress with it and are hoping to have cracked it reasonably soon.'

'Good. Yes, that is, indeed, interesting. Can you put everything else aside, please, and just focus on this one thing?'

Gloria glanced at Ben who just shrugged and then said, 'Yes, I suppose so.'

'Thanks. Now for the rest of you. Dennis, Lucy and Geoffrey. I want you guys to see if anyone has purchased a ship big enough to cross the ocean in and launch a couple of nuclear missiles from in, say, the last year or so. Start with the Lloyd's Registry. I know there will probably be hundreds but I reckon we'll be able to eliminate most of them quite quickly. Focus on freighters first. I'm thinking that, if we can identify the vessel, this could be an important breakthrough which we can pass on to our political masters. I hope you agree. I know it's going to be tedious work but I'd like it done. My gut's telling me the ship is out there and I need confirmation.

OK?' And they all nodded. 'The other two of you, Alan and Felicity, I'd like to operate as a kind of think tank to come up with solutions, however esoteric, of how we might be able to neutralise the ship with extreme stealth, without setting off the nuclear weapons. OK? Look on it as good mental exercise and don't be afraid to think outside the box. By the way, I expect Toby is focussing on where the missiles come from, if they actually exist. Which brings me to my last point: I apologise in advance if this is all a wild goose chase but it sure is important enough to warrant checking out. We'll all meet back here at 5 pm. Go to it, guys and remember this is an absolute priority. You can put all your usual work on the back burner.' And with that exhortation ringing in their ears, they left to get on with their different tasks.

One thing I'd said which came out off the cuff was about Toby and I decided to ring him first when I got back to the office. He answered quickly and I asked whether my guess at the meeting about what he was probably doing to help was true. 'Yes, you're absolutely right on the money, Jack. We are, indeed, looking into where the missiles might have come from, and have already made some progress on that score. One of our highest-level contacts in Russia has just told us that two of their missiles appear to have gone missing on a train journey from a nuclear arsenal near Moscow for re-assignment in the Far East. But the Russians are keeping very quiet about it, which neither confirms nor denies the possibility of state sponsorship. They might of course just be embarrassed. But we'll keep digging and try to get some proof either way.'

'Good man! That was quick work!'

'Yes, I thought so too. Our contact just happened to be in the right place at the right time. More good luck than good management, I confess. What have you guys been up to?'

So I gave him a quick rundown on everything my team had just told me. 'But it's all horribly circumstantial. No hard facts that I can present to the politicos.'

'True,' he muttered. Then he asked if I'd managed to get the satellite I'd been about to ask for the day before. I'd forgotten I'd mentioned that to him and told him about a possible delay there but that it should be resolved pretty soon.

'Good luck with that. Every time I've asked for satellite surveillance of a suspect, unless it was in a fully-fledged war zone, I've always been given the run-around. Well, I suppose we do have a little time and we've been down to the wire before now, haven't we?'

'Yes, true,' I said grimly. And we said our goodbyes and hung up.

Now I knew it was time to bring Sir M up to date and that I needed to do this in person. So I gathered my notes and went up to his magnificent top-floor office with its glorious view of the river. He was in as I'd suspected he would be. If something big was happening, he always liked to be at the centre of things, even at the age of seventy five. He was surrounded by all my files and I wondered flippantly if I could ask for a raise when this was all over now that he knew what I did for a living.

'Hello, Jack!' he boomed. 'Have you come to save me from drowning in paper?' waving his hands at the files littering his normally pristine desk.

'Not exactly, Sir,' I said. 'But we are making some progress.' And I proceeded to give him an update on where we were now. He listened in silence and I concluded, 'I know it's all circumstantial but you must admit the evidence for *something* afoot is starting to build up. I reckon it's all down to finding this ship, if it, indeed, exists.'

'Yes, I guess it is,' he said pensively. 'And, on that score, how's that satellite going you wanted? I hope Sir Philip was useful.'

'Oh, yes, I forgot to mention that. Yes, as useful as he could be, anyway. He said there might be a delay getting one of ours in position but that he might ask the Americans if we could borrow one of theirs.'

'Good. Well, you seem to be doing everything you can. Keep up the good work and keep me informed.'

Praise, indeed, coming from him. I knew he would have reminded me (probably brutally) if I'd forgotten anything crucial. I left him and went back to my own office. I looked at my watch and saw it was now 11.00. A good time I reckoned to contact Sir Philip and find out what was going on.

'Hello, Mr Sanderson. I was wondering if you might call,' he said when I got through. 'The answer to your obvious question is that I'm making progress although it's probably a little slower than you would have wished. I obviously tried our own resources first but, as I suspected, they're all tied up watching the Russian border, the Iranians and the North Koreans. It would take quite a while to get one of them re-positioned so I went cap in hand to the Americans. I spoke to my opposite number there who owes us a favour or two and, after I'd stressed the urgency of the situation and how it was under the direct aegis of our PM, he agreed to lend us one of theirs. It should be in position by about this time tomorrow, he told me. It shouldn't take more than about 12 hours to cover the quadrant you gave me as it's quite small so by this time on Friday evening you should have your answer. And that's quick, let me tell you.'

'That's good, Sir Philip. Thank you very much. At least it gives us a time frame we can work within. Will you have access to the live feed?'

'It wouldn't be me, more likely to be GCHQ in Cheltenham. I'd have to go back to the Americans and ask them to send it straight to them.'

'Would you do that, please? It's very important that I can see any ships in the quadrant with my own eyes.'

'Certainly. That's not a problem. The hard part's been done, actually getting the satellite. The rest is quite straightforward.'

'That's great!' I said enthusiastically. 'Thank you very much indeed, Sir.'

'My pleasure. Always happy to help the Security Services. I'll get onto my opposite number over the other side of the pond straight away.'

'I believe you've just done your country a very important service.' And with those final words and a few more pleasantries on both sides, I disconnected.

I knew what I had to do now, get in touch with GCHQ (*the main government intelligence gathering facility*) and tell them what was going on, although not all of it. So I rang Ted Fisher, the Director of the place who I'd had dealings with before and liked a lot, after looking up his number in my address book.

'Hello, Ted. How are you?' I asked when I'd got through the multiple levels of security surrounding him.

'Hello, Jack. I guess this isn't a social call and you've got a problem.'

'Yes, you're right. Potentially a very serious one. I've just got off the phone with Sir Philip Larkin, who you must know.' I paused and he grunted agreement before I continued. 'He has got the Americans to lend us one of their spy satellites which I need to survey a quadrant of about 10,000 square kilometres in the mid-Atlantic. I'm looking for a vessel of a particular sort which could pose a real threat to the security of the whole country. He told me it should be in position about 24 hours from now and ready to start beaming back live video footage then. I asked him if he could ask the Americans to send the footage straight to you guys at GCHQ and he said yes, that shouldn't be a problem. My question for you, apart from warning you the footage is on the way, is, would it be possible for me to watch it live here in London or do I have to come to Cheltenham?'

'It's very unusual for us to send live footage out of

this building. It would, I think, depend on the level of security surrounding it. So, for example, is it top secret? And do you guys have the facilities to watch it there, bearing in mind that it will probably be encrypted?'

'OK, Ted. You've convinced me. Yes, it is top secret. I'll come to Cheltenham. Can you set up a camp bed or something on the premises? I don't expect to be staying long, probably no more than about 12 hours, provided that the technology all works.'

He laughed and said, 'We can do better than that. So when can we expect you?'

'How about lunch time tomorrow? Oh, and I'll probably be bringing my aide-de-camp.'

'So we're going to have to feed and house two of you,' he said, laughing again. 'Yes, of course. That's fine. I'll see you tomorrow. We can catch up over lunch.'

'Looking forward to it already. Thanks, Ted.' And, after saying bye, I disconnected. Looking at my watch again, I saw it was now 12.00 and the executive canteen would be open. My stomach was growling and I knew I needed food. Apart from anything else, I thought better when I was eating.

So I made my way up there on the top floor and had a decent meal, uninterrupted by anyone except for the waiters who were actually very discreet. And I did manage to do some decent thinking, most of it fairly gloomy. What would I do if this was all a storm in a tea cup? There would have to be multiple apologies, that was for sure, all the way up the ladder. But I reminded myself that my intuitions were rarely wrong, especially in an important case like this, and I felt in my gut that something untoward was about to happen. ISIS had been very quiet recently but I knew they were still out there, as fanatical as ever.

CHAPTER 6

THURSDAY PM

Back in the office again, the first thing I had to do was to update Sir M on what was going on with the satellite and the fact that I'd be going to Cheltenham on the morrow, which I did quite quickly over the phone. Then I had an idea and called Toby.

'Hey, Toby, old son?' I said by way of introduction. 'How do you fancy a journey out of the smoke? I have to go to Cheltenham tomorrow morning to watch some live satellite footage and I'll need some company. I was thinking of taking Alan but I think, on second thoughts, he can be better employed here.'

'Why don't you just fess up and say you need a driver?'

'There is that too of course,' I said, grinning down the phone at his turn of phrase. 'But, seriously, I thought you might be interested in seeing whether this wretched ship actually exists.'

'Yes, of course I'm interested. What time do you want to meet?'

'How about 8.30? That should get us there in plenty of time to watch the action.'

'OK. I'll pick you up at your place then. Your flat, I mean.'

'Thanks, Toby. See you then.' And I hung up, pleased that I'd thought of inviting him. And it *was* important to keep Alan here. Now, what else did I have to do? I could think of nothing earth-shatteringly important and decided to get down to sorting out my notes and putting them in some kind of order. This took me about an hour and a half and it was about 4pm by the time I'd finished. Reading them through had reminded me of something I'd said at the COBRA meeting and I made a note to mention it to Toby tomorrow. I was feeling restless now and knew I still had another hour to go before my meeting with the team so I decided to go and check on Gloria and Ben who I knew had the best chance of having achieved something by now.

So I toddled downstairs to Gloria's office where I knew they'd be working and found them surrounded by seemingly hundreds of bits of computer equipment and paper. They both looked rather frazzled around the edges and I remembered guiltily that they'd probably been up most of the previous night. 'Any progress, guys?' I asked after barging in. They brightened up when they saw me and Ben said, 'Yes, actually. Gloria finally got into the bank through a back door and we're just getting the payments in and out of the account now. And some of them are pretty staggering.'

I came over to their work station and peered over their shoulders at the columns of numbers on the screen. He pointed at two, one for $15 million which went out nearly a year ago, I noticed, and the other for about $124 million which left the account about 6 months ago. 'I wonder if one of the payments could be for the missiles and one for the ship,' I mused.

Gloria said now, 'Yes, we had the same idea. Now all we have to do is identify the recipients – oh, and the sender. I'm afraid we still haven't managed to identify who the account belongs to. That will take longer. But we'll get there eventually.'

'Good work!' I said enthusiastically. 'Now we've got something a bit more concrete to show the guys who are looking for the ship. Maybe it'll help them. By the way, I'd like to order you both to go home and get a good night's sleep after the meeting tonight and come in tomorrow all bright-eyes and bushy-tailed. You're both looking bush-whacked. This can keep.'

'Thank you, sir,' they both chorused. 'We'll do that,' added Gloria. 'We are rather tired, it's true.' And with that I left them.

Then I went up to the conference room and put what we knew or suspected up on the board in the time order we'd found it out. And, looking at it, I realised how much progress we'd already made. Then I just sat back and waited for everybody to turn up. They all arrived shortly after and I noticed them all avidly reading what I'd put on the board. I let them all assimilate it and then said, 'Anybody got anything to add?'

Geoffrey spoke up first. 'You were right, sir, when you said it'd be tedious work looking for a single ship which has been bought over the past year. There are, indeed, hundreds registered just at Lloyds but I think we've managed to narrow it down quite a lot.'

'Thanks, Geoffrey, Lucy and Dennis. That's the most I could have expected. But I think Gloria and Ben may be able to help you a bit here. Gloria, would you like to summarise what you've just found out?' And as she did so, I added the details to the board.

'Thanks, guys,' Dennis said now, 'that could, indeed, be very helpful in assisting us to narrow down the search.'

'But don't take it as gospel,' Gloria warned.

'And so, finally, we come to Alan and Felicity's brainstorming session? Did you two manage to come up with anything feasible?'

'We think so but we're not sure. It depends on the technology available,' Alan said. 'One idea is to send a mini stealth submarine under the ship to attach limpet mines to the hull. Another involves a sub or warship standing some way off ready to fire anti-ballistic missiles, just in case they manage to fire the two pulse weapons. And an idea we had about getting onto the ship legitimately. What about sending a navy ship out to it, saying that it had some intelligence about a crew member having a bunch of illegal drugs and could they search it. If they said no, we reckon that could prove there was something fishy about it.' And here he paused.

'Hmm. You're not asking for much, are you? Do mini stealth submarines actually exist? But I do quite like your last idea,' I said now.

'We're pretty sure they're at least in development in the USA,' Felicity said. 'There was an article in one of the

Defence Journals about them. Apparently the Germans invented the idea in World War 2 and the SOE used a similar idea in Norway to attack German warships in heavily defended harbours.'

'I must have missed that,' I said. 'OK. At least I have something to present to the Joint Chiefs if it comes to the crunch. Thanks for that, guys.' And I added their ideas to the board. 'Now you all must be wondering what I've been up to. Well, I got us a satellite, an American one, to be precise.' And a cheer went up from all present. 'It should be in position by about 11am tomorrow morning and I've been told that an entire sweep of the quadrant shouldn't take more than about 12 hours. The only problem is that the footage will be beamed to GCHQ so I'm going to have to go there, leaving early tomorrow. So I'm going to have to leave you in Alan's capable hands all day tomorrow. Oh, yes, and I'll be taking Toby with me. I've been keeping him updated with our progress and him with me likewise. Hence the comment on the board about the missing missiles.'

'Now then, what can you lot be doing tomorrow? Unless anyone has a better idea, I'd like you all to continue what you've been doing. Remember Dennis, Lucy and Geoffrey, I'm basically looking for the names of suitable candidate ships. Maybe you can focus just on vessels that cost around 124 million dollars. That should narrow it down a lot. If I'm successful tomorrow of course, all your hard work will just be more confirmation but this is important if I'm to convince the politicos that ISIS / Al Qaeda have a case to answer. Maybe, Felicity, you could join them. Many hands make light work and all that. Meanwhile, Ben and Gloria, I'd be grateful if you two could continue trying to find out who the hell owns this bloody bank account. Follow the money, I always say. Alan, that just leaves you. I'd like you to be a floating voter, helping out where needed and keeping in close contact with me.'

'Yes, boss,' he said.

'And if anyone would like to offer up a prayer for success in Cheltenham tomorrow, that wouldn't go amiss. Now I want everyone to go home and get a decent night's sleep. I don't want any of you to be in before 9 tomorrow, OK?' There was another cheer at this and I knew I'd managed to keep them all onside.

I went back to my office then and called Pamela, saying I'd be back soon. Then I just packed my notes in my briefcase and my laptop away in my safe and set off for home. When I got back, I told Pamela that it was very possible that I might be away all night tomorrow as I had to go to Cheltenham with Toby. She took this news resignedly and didn't ask any questions, for which I was grateful. Then, after another of her decent dinners, I went straight to bed, slipping almost at once, in spite of my worry that I might be putting all my eggs in one basket, into the arms of Morpheus.

CHAPTER 7

FRIDAY AM

I was picked up the next morning by Toby at 8.30 as we'd agreed and set off for Cheltenham. We talked a bit on the way, Toby being remarkably positive about the case and I told him the ideas my team had come up with. He ruminated a while before saying, 'Yes, I like the idea of using drugs as a pretext to search the vessel. And I think that their ideas to take out the ship might just work. But I'd be worried in case the ship does have a submersible. What would happen if it was on duty 24/7?'

'Something we'll just have to take into account, I guess,' I said, pleased that he'd put finger directly on the weak spot in the idea of using a mini stealth submarine, something I'd thought of during Alan's presentation but hadn't spoken about as I didn't want to dash their enthusiasm. 'What are you guys working on?'

'Basically, we're now trying to make a list of who in ISIS or Al-Qaeda has the intelligence to plan an operation like this and power to carry it out without anyone getting wind of it. And it looks like being a very short list indeed. And they are all, as far as we know, holed up in the mountains of Pakistan.'

'Good man,' I said. 'I'd almost forgotten the mastermind behind it all until I was re-reading my notes yesterday afternoon and I made a note to ask you to look into that.'

'We're obviously way ahead of you,' he said with a grin but I didn't rise to his joshing and simply turned the conversation to family matters.

It was quite a pleasant journey, except for the nightmare of the M25 and getting past Heathrow, and we reached our destination at about 10.30. GCHQ seemed to have increased in size since I was last here a couple of years ago with yet more radomes visible stretching away into the distance and more office blocks. Even though I'd told them Ted Foster was expecting us, the guards at the formidable barricades checked our passes carefully and did a quick but professional sweep of the car before letting us through with one of them accompanying us to one of the tallest blocks before handing us over to another guard. He took us inside the building and told reception that Mr Foster's two guests were here. We were told to sit in the waiting area until somebody came to collect us.

But it wasn't just anybody. It was Ted Foster himself. He walked across the huge foyer to where we were sitting and I looked up from my notes to see him standing in front of me. 'Hello, Jack. Welcome to my humble abode,' he said humorously. I jumped up and held out my hand which he shook vigorously. 'And Toby too, I am honoured and humbled. Jack didn't tell me he was bringing you too.' I'd forgotten that Ted knew Toby and watched as they shook hands. Then he said, 'Why don't you both follow me?'

We followed him to an elevator and descended to a sub-basement far underground. On the way he said, 'Your problem must be serious to bring both of you here.'

'Potentially very serious. I just hope I'm not wasting everybody's time,' I said.

'I thought I'd take you straight down to where you'll be working so as not to waste *your* time.'

'Thanks, Ted,' I said. We passed a lot of rooms with their doors closed and finally reached a huge operations room, which needed its door opened with a handprint and optical scanner like the COBRA room. It had multiple screens all displaying different scenes from around the world with many technicians operating the computers on the desks in front of them. It looked like a set from a James Bond film.

'This is where all our satellite stuff comes into,' Ted told us although that much was obvious. He walked around the room with us following dutifully until he came to another door and this one just opened with a normal handle. We walked into what seemed to be a smallish office with a computer with a large screen sitting on a desk and a couple of comfortable–looking office chairs behind the one directly in front of the computer technician who was operating the system. There was nothing else on the desk except for a telephone. The room had off-white walls and a reddish carpet and that was it. Nothing remarkable about it at all.

I looked again at the technician and noticed to my surprise that it was a young Asian woman. I shouldn't have been surprised – Gloria, after all, was also young and possibly the best hacker in the country – but I guess I'm a bit of an old fogey when it comes to top secret jobs. Ted introduced us now to Karen as "our two honoured guests from MI5 and MI6, Jack and Toby" and told us that Karen was one his best operatives. 'She's on loan to you for as long as you need her. But I'll want her back I'm afraid.' He said this last sentence with a grin and we both grinned back at him. I wondered whether he knew how many of our best people had been poached from other government departments and even the private sector.

'OK. Does that mean we can't give her our recruitment spiel?' I said as I shook hands with her.

'You can try, I guess,' he said, grinning himself now. 'But enough of this frivolity. I know you've got work to do so I'll leave you now. Get in touch as soon as you're ready to eat. I've got a table booked upstairs and a nice flat available for you both if you need to spend the night.'

'Many thanks, Ted. OK, we'll see you later then.' And then he left in a whirlwind of energy.

Now Toby spoke up, 'Do you know where the nearest gents is, Karen? We've had a long drive.'

'Didn't Ted show you? That's typical of him. Yes, indeed. Follow me. So we followed her out of the little office back into the huge open area where everyone seemed to be incredibly busy and to the other side where I spotted a sign saying "Gentlemen".

'OK. We can take it from here, Karen, thanks,' Toby said.

'Can I get you guys some coffee? I'll bet Ted didn't think of that either,' she asked. 'Yes, please,' we chorused. And she left us after taking our orders. We both went into the loos and did our business, giving our faces and hands a good wash in warm water, then strolled back to our little room where cups of decent coffee awaited us.

'That's much better,' I told her, swallowing the last mouthful. 'Now to work. What's the state of play with our satellite, Karen?'

'It should be coming on line very soon now,' she said, pointing at a little clock in the corner of her screen which was counting down the minutes. I looked at my watch – 11.10. 'Very efficient,' I said.

'Yes. It seems like the Americans have pulled out all the stops for you guys. Can you tell me a little more about your operation? All I really know is that you're looking for a ship. Any particular kind?'

'All we can tell you is that we'll know it if we find it,' I said. 'Can you communicate directly with the satellite's controllers in the USA?'

'Yes, of course. If you need to see more in close up, just tell me and I'll ask them.'

'That's great. It's all I could have hoped for,' I said now.

Then the computer screen woke up to a vista of grey and an American voice saying, 'There you go, GCHQ. You should be receiving signals now. Good luck. We hope you find what you're looking for.' And I realised that the grey on the screen was actually the ocean.

'Can you ask them exactly how they're going to scan the quadrant we gave them?' I asked. 'I mean, are they going to start in the centre and work out from there or what?'

'Our clients want to know how you're going to do the scanning, Fort Meade,' Karen asked now, speaking into a small microphone attached to her lapel I hadn't noticed before. 'Are you going to use diagonals as usual?'

'Yes, we reckon that's probably the fastest way to scan the whole quadrant. You should now be looking at a patch of empty ocean from the upper right corner of the quadrant.'

'And how long will it take to get to the centre?'

'Not long. About a couple of hours we reckon.'

'Can you ask them finally if they can themselves keep an eye out for any ships, especially ones that are stationary or seem to be moving in circles, and mark their exact positions so that they can take us back to them in case we miss them?'

'I think they'll do that anyway. They know you're looking for a ship and not a specific one in this area but I'll do it anyway.'

'Thanks, Karen. I would hate to miss it if it's there,' I said. So she relayed my message and got a cheerful 'Will do,' in response.

'Thanks again, Karen, one final question for you rather than them. Would we be allowed to ask them questions ourselves? I don't want to have to keep you away from your regular duties too long.'

'I'm afraid not. It's all voiceprint controlled as an extra security measure. So you're stuck with me for the duration. Sorry about that. But it's nice of you to think of me.' She gave me a big grin now and I suddenly realised just how attractive she was.

'OK. Fair enough. But if we're going to be stuck in here for the next 12 hours, can I ask you something?'

'Ask away.'

'How did you get into this game? Presumably it's pretty difficult to work in this place and even more difficult to work your way up to a position of trust like you obviously have.'

'So you want a potted CV. Sure. Many years ago when I was still a teenager, I managed to hack my way into 'this place', as you call it, and was sent to prison. However, Ted Foster was so impressed with my computer skills that he got me out and used me for a while to improve their security here. And when I'd done that, to my and his satisfaction, I moved sideways into the satellite job I have now. I like it. It's stimulating and suits my temperament. And that's it.'

'Thanks for being so honest. It's almost exactly what happened to my own best computer expert. And she's probably even younger than you. But she was into hacking banks,' I mused.

All this time while we'd been conversing, Toby had been concentrating on the screen in front of us, not saying anything but listening to our conversation with one ear.

'Karen, watch out for Jack,' he said. 'When he's in a poaching mood, he can be ruthless.' But then he suddenly changed tack. 'Look, guys! There's a ship on the screen.'

He was right. There was! It was just coming into view as it headed across the quadrant. I could see its wake quite clearly and reckoned it was going at quite a clip. The weather, fortunately, was quite clear. It had a white superstructure, I noticed now, and looked like a tourist liner. Now would be a good time to concentrate on work.

I said to Karen, 'Can you ask the Americans to zoom in close? I'd like to see how good their satellite technology is these days.' She relayed my request to them and within a few seconds it felt like I was standing next to someone on deck! It was a woman, I could see, and her hair was blowing in the breeze. She was dressed in shorts and a T-shirt and had on white trainers. She looked like a tourist. 'Can you ask them now if they can get the name of the ship? This is really crucial as we'll need the names of all ships in the quadrant.' She relayed this and again very quickly we could see it clearly. It was called 'Aurora' and from the stern it obviously was a tourist liner and a big one too. It was part of the Cunard fleet and was probably taking tourists from New York to London. What we have to do to make the world safe for types like those, I thought sourly. I was a bit disheartened that this wasn't our ship but knew there would inevitably be disappointments. There are plenty more fish in the sea, I told myself. 'OK. Tell them thank you. I'm most impressed by the clarity of the images but it's not ours. They can go back to usual scanning.' And again very quickly the satellite pulled its cameras back and we were watching the featureless ocean beneath us.

We watched the ocean for about another 40 minutes or so and my stomach was starting to growl. I knew I'd have to eat soon or I'd completely lose concentration. But then Karen's sharp eyes spotted something. 'What's that?' she said. I looked carefully and saw it was definitely a ship but it seemed to be painted battle-ship grey and was almost invisible against the grey of the ocean as if it was camouflaged. And it didn't seem to be moving! At least there was no wake behind it. 'Ask the Americans to pull their cameras into it,' I said urgently. She did so and again they performed their miracle and I was watching a scene of obviously controlled chaos on deck. There were a number of seamen all busy guiding what looked like a giant cable out of the sea. As they pulled it out, it was being wound onto a giant drum. 'I think it's just a cable laying vessel or perhaps a cable repairing one,' she said now.

And I remembered how there were many undersea cables connecting America and Europe and felt disappointed all over again. But then Toby spoke up with a note of excitement in his voice, 'Can you ask them to pull the camera back just a little so we can see the whole deck?' And she did so. Then he said, 'Unless I'm very much mistaken, isn't that a submersible on the foredeck? And didn't you say something about submersibles on the way up here, Jack?' 'Yes, indeed I did,' I replied, getting excited all over again. 'Can you ask them to get the name of the ship?' I asked Karen, trying to sound nonchalant but not really succeeding. They changed the position of the camera and now it was pointing directly at the stern where I saw the name 'Virago' emblazoned on it in what looked like new paint. 'Can they now scan the whole ship slowly again, please?' I asked and I saw the cameras moving again but very slowly this time. It was definitely a freighter of some description, about the size of what I'd imagined, and it looked as if it had all been recently re-painted.

Its most obvious feature was the large helipad attached by strong stanchions to the ship's stern but I ignored this after I realised that all such vessels probably needed one of those if they were going to be re-supplied quickly after being stuck in mid-ocean for weeks doing their job. Another obvious feature was the huge derricks on the decks. However, I had a feeling in my gut about this ship but knew that I couldn't talk about it in front of Karen. 'Can we see a picture of the master of the vessel if that's possible?' I said now. 'Probably not,' came back the reply in a few seconds. 'It's usually very difficult to see through the glass on the bridge. But we can try.' And the camera panned out and then in again looking straight at the window of the bridge. He was right, unfortunately. We could see nothing at all through the glass, especially as the sun was shining and reflecting straight off it. 'OK,' I said now. 'How about an officer, then?' And again the camera panned back until the whole deck was in view. And my intuition paid off. There was an officer supervising the men working on the cable but he was wearing a peaked cap pulled down over his eyes and appeared to have a beard and moustache. He was also wearing sunglasses which would make it very difficult to identify him. But not impossible, I thought. 'Ask them if they can send us a still picture of that man. And, for that matter, still pictures of everything else we've seen of the ship.' And the friendly American voice said 'Yes, sure. They should be with you in a few minutes.' Then I thought of something else. 'Does the ship have a flag to show where it was registered?' Now the cameras panned up to above the bridge where there was an obvious British ensign flying. 'OK. Many thanks, Fort Meade. That'll do for the moment. You can carry on scanning the ocean for any other ships but first can you tell me the exact coordinates of this one?' 'Yes, sure,' he said again and rattled them off. I copied them into my notebook, and then I noticed they were up there in the corner of the screen and felt rather foolish. But my pride could wait. I wanted to talk to Toby and to do that I'd have to get out of this little room. So I said, 'Let's go and have that lunch Ted promised us.' He promptly caught on to my tone of voice and said, 'Yeah, sure. That's a good idea.'

'I presume you're taping everything, Karen?'

'Of course. We're not complete morons, you know,' she said with a grin and I knew I was forgiven. 'I won't be going anywhere and I'm certain that Fort Meade will catch me up on anything I miss.'

'Thanks a lot, Karen. See you soon.' And with that, we left.

CHAPTER 8

FRIDAY PM

On the way up in the elevator I asked Toby, 'So what do you think? Do you reckon it's a likely candidate?'

He answered slowly, 'Yes, I think so. I presume you noticed the huge array of antennas sprouting out of the top of the bridge? I think there were too many for an ordinary cable laying ship. But what do I know?'

'Yes, I did. And I presume *you* noticed the large structure on the foredeck covered with tarpaulin? Big enough for a couple of smallish missiles, do you think? But what do I know?' I said, echoing his own semi-humorous words. 'I think we've got something now we can get our teeth into.'

'Yes, I agree. All we need now is confirmation that it's not a bona-fide cable-laying ship which shouldn't be too difficult to get.'

'It's a clever idea for disguise if it's not. Nobody would normally look twice at it.'

'Yes. I thought of that.'

'I'm glad we're in agreement. Now I think we need a

secure phone line so we can call our respective teams and ask them to look into it.'

'And I'm sure this place has a plethora of those,' he said now.

And there we had to leave it as we were coming out of the otherwise empty lift and into the huge foyer. We asked the receptionist if she could call up to Ted, who was presumably still in his office, and she did so. She handed the phone to me when he replied saying, 'So are you two getting hungry?'

'Yes, absolutely,' I answered for both of us. 'There is, however, one more thing we need before we eat.'

'Oh yes, what's that?' he said.

'An absolutely secure phone line, please.'

'Sure. You can ring from my office. Come on up. I'll tell the guard on the lift you're on your way. The 18th floor, remember, Jack?'

'We'll just follow the Titians and the Aubussons, OK?'

He laughed and hung up. The receptionist who had been listening in to this banter directed us to the appropriate lift and we were whisked up to the top floor after the guard had looked at our cards and checked our names off on his list. We got out to face a stunning panoramic view through huge plate glass windows of the whole site and my memory told us to turn left. We walked down a longish corridor and ended up in front of a large door. There was more security rigmarole before his secretary let us in and then we were inside Ted's own imposing corner office.

Ted was sitting behind a large but government-issue

desk which had a lot of papers on it and talking on the phone. He waved us in and we sat in a couple of comfortable arm chairs in front of him. I looked around and was impressed by the lack of obvious luxury. A few nicely-framed photos on the wall of him meeting famous people and that was about it. He soon finished his call and asked us straight out, 'Any luck, then?'

'Possibly,' I told him. 'But we'll have to do a lot more digging before we're sure.'

'And that's why you need my phone?' he asked cannily now.

'Exactly,' I said.

'OK. I'll leave you in peace and toddle off to the executive dining room. I'll wait for you there. Hope you're not going to be too long. It's one floor below this one.'

'No, we shouldn't be. And yes, I remember now. We'll find it.'

'Oh, and if you don't want my secretary listening in to your call, remember to press this red button here.'

'Thanks Ted. Are you sure I won't start a nuclear war by pressing the red button?'

'Ever the joker, aren't you, Jack?' he said laughing.

'Only when the situation warrants it,' I replied. And he laughed again before walking out. 'OK, Toby, I think I'll ring Sir M and brief him. He should be able to easily get hold of Alan and pass on the information. That way I'll kill two birds with one stone. Then you can have your go.'

'Yes, good thinking,' Toby said.

So I did that, telling him the name of the ship we were

interested in and its co-ordinates and the reasons for our interest and not forgetting to say that we'd be coming back to London armed with bunches of photos which I'd pass on to Alan at the first opportunity. I finished by saying, 'I've got a feeling about this one, Sir.' And he replied by saying, 'That's good enough for me, Jack,' and I was grateful for his support. I didn't need to tell him to pass everything on to Alan ASAP as I knew he'd do that automatically.

Then it was Toby's turn and I listened in to his half of the conversation, wondering what I'd forgotten to tell Sir M, but it didn't seem there was anything important. I looked at my watch now and saw it was 1.10pm, a good time to eat, especially as I was starving now. We'd only been in Ted's office about 30 minutes but I wondered if Ted had already started. So we sauntered down, talking about the case on the way. I was particularly keen to get back to London now and I asked him if he felt the same. 'Yes,' he said. 'Empty ocean doesn't do much to help my concentration. I certainly hope this is our ship but I too feel it probably is.'

'Shall we leave straight after lunch?' I asked.

'Perhaps we should spend a while longer with the delectable Karen just to confuse the issue a bit.'

'Yes. OK,' I said, realising he was right but not so sure about his sexist use of the language. But I decided to ignore it as there was no one else within earshot and Toby and I were old pals. We soon reached the executive dining room where we met Ted who didn't seem particularly phased by our tardiness and had a lovely lunch but

I wasn't surprised by this, thinking of all the world's bigwigs who had passed through here. Ted tried gently to pump us for information about what we were up to but we managed to deflect his interest, just saying, 'If we're right about our suspicions, you'll be put in the loop sooner rather than later, we suspect.' And he had to be content with that. Apart from that, we mainly talked about personal stuff – I hadn't had a chance to do this for about 18 months and for Toby it was even longer. We just stuck to water, no alcohol, and the lunch didn't last very long. Then, just before we split up, I said, 'We'll probably be returning to London fairly soon after a bit more work with Karen. So we won't be needing your kind offer of that flat.'

'Oh, that's OK. You know you and Toby are always welcome guests here,' he said. 'I'll ring down to the ops room and tell them to expect you.' Then we went our different ways, us returning to the operations room and our little office where Karen was waiting for us.

'I hope you managed to get some lunch,' I said to her.

'Yes, thanks. I brought a sandwich with me,' she said. 'Did you enjoy yours?'

'Yes, indeed,' I replied. 'Has there been any excitement since our cable laying ship?'

'No, not really. A fleet of trawlers went by not long ago, loaded with fish and obviously heading back to port in the USA. And that's about it. And to answer your next question: yes, I got all their names. Why did you have to choose such an empty stretch of sea to watch?'

'We like boring Ted's employees to death,' I said which made her laugh. 'Have you got those pictures for us?'

'Sure do,' she replied, handing me a couple of large sealed packs of papers. 'I took the liberty of making two sets, one for each of you.'

'Thanks ever so much, Karen. I can see why Ted treasures you so highly,' Toby said now which actually made her blush.

'We think we won't stay much longer but you said earlier that you're making a copy of everything America is sending you. When the satellite finishes its passes over the quadrant, can you make 2 copies of that also and send one of them to me at MI5 and another to Toby at MI6. We'll need to show all the footage, preferably minus the empty ocean, to our teams. If you could send them by priority courier tonight, that would be great. Time really is of the essence for us,' I said.

'Of course. Your wish is my command, oh honoured sir,' she said now with another of her infectious grins. And I knew it would happen.

'Thanks ever so much,' and I'd rarely said anything so honestly in my life. Then we sat around staring at the empty ocean for about another half an hour until I signalled Toby who got up, stretched and said, 'I reckon that's about all I can handle for one day.' I got up too and held out my hand to Karen, saying, 'Don't forget, Karen. If you ever need a change of direction, you know where we are. Also remember that everything you saw here today is absolutely top secret. So no talking about any of it in the bar. As I told Ted, you'll all be put in the loop sooner rather than later if my suspicions prove correct.'

'Thanks, guys. But I'm happy enough here. See you around. And yes, my lips are sealed.'

And with that we left the office and went back to the car, although we did have a little trouble taking the packets of documents out of the building which needed another call to Ted to sort out. Then it was off back to London. It was now about 3.00 and I was worried I might not make it back for my 5pm meeting with the team. I told Toby this and he put his siren on the roof and really tore back to London, breaking the speed limit all the way. We talked a little on the way, mainly agreeing on what each of our teams could do so we wouldn't be duplicating each other too much. I also skimmed the photos in the package and was amazed once again by their clarity. They reminded me to ask him to focus his efforts on trying to identify the officer in the photos and he said he would. When we arrived at MI5's headquarters just before 5.00, I rushed in after thanking Toby effusively for his speed and saying, 'Keep in touch.'

I went up to my office first and rang Alan to tell him I'd be along to the meeting shortly, then had a quick wash and brush up. Then it was back to the conference room where everyone was assembled. There seemed to be an atmosphere of excitement in the air and I wondered if they had some news for me already. So right off I asked them and Alan spoke up for them all saying, 'Yes, we think so, sir. I'll let Gloria go first.'

'Well, we finally managed to crack that bloody

bank account and you'll never guess where it seemed to originate.'

'Surprise me,' I said.

'The Kremlin,' she said with a big grin. 'However, you need to take our findings with a pinch of salt. It'll probably never be provable in a court of law but all the evidence points that way and that's good enough for us.'

'Good grief,' I said. 'So it is being state sponsored. That bloody Putin up to his old tricks. When he failed to get everything his own way in Ukraine, he decides to take the law into his own hands again and get his revenge through a proxy.'

'Yes, that's the way we read it.'

'This will have to go right to the top and pronto,' I said now. 'OK, well done, guys. Have the rest of you got any news about that bloody ship we found?'

'Yes, we think so,' Alan said. 'It seems that the Virago left Liverpool a few weeks ago to do some cable repairs in the North Atlantic somewhere before heading off to Abu Dhabi. We got onto it through the money even before your phone call alerting us about Virago. Apparently it cost roughly $124 million.'

'Liverpool, eh?' I said. 'That's one of the things I've been worrying about. A direct English connection. Perhaps the mastermind behind the plan is here right now. OK, guys, very good work. Now I think you all need to be putting your energies into finding this mastermind. Concentrate on Russians in the first place. I think it's got to be a Russian. I was talking to Toby about this and he told me that there were very few members of ISIS or Al-Qaeda capable of planning such a sophisticated operation and those were all holed up in the mountains of Pakistan. But if it's being planned by Russia, it puts a whole different complexion on the case. Now, before you all go home and get some sleep, I've got a few photos to show you.' And I proceeded to fan them out on the table so everybody could get a good look at them. Once they'd done that, I asked for comments and Dennis spoke up.

'I think I can understand why you were so concerned about this particular ship. First, there's the big array of aerials on the top of the superstructure which makes it look as if it could communicate with anybody anywhere very fast. And second, there's the large structure on the foredeck which could house a couple of medium range missiles.'

'Our own thoughts exactly. Thank you, Dennis. Anybody got anything to add?'

And Lucy said, 'There's also a submersible in full view on the deck. But it's all pretty circumstantial, isn't it?

'Yes, that was what first made Toby suspicious. And I agree it's not conclusive. But remember, we're dealing with the balance of probabilities here. But thanks anyway, Lucy. And something's just occurred to me. I'll need a couple of you to check out the crew roster for the ship. If it left from Liverpool, that shouldn't be too difficult. We need more information about who we're dealing with. And we also need to find out who the new owner is of course. Indeed, any more information about the Virago would be very welcome. Maybe first thing tomorrow you two, Alan and Lucy, could be getting on with that.'

'Yes, boss,' they chorused.

'Ok, thanks again, guys. Now I've got something a bit more definitive, I'm ready to go back upstairs. See you all in here at 9am.'

So they all left to sort out their priorities while I added the new information I'd received today to the board as well as putting up the pictures around the room. Then I went up to Sir M's office and brought him up to date. He was horrified by the Russian connection as I knew he would be and promised he'd get through to the PM as soon as I left. There was just one thing left to do now: ring Toby. I got hold of him quickly once down in my office and told him the latest and what I'd tasked my team to do tomorrow. 'Thanks for all that,' he said pensively when I'd finished. 'I reckon I'm not that surprised. The Russians have always been devious bastards, at least on the geopolitical stage.' And there we left it.

There was one more tiny little thing I wanted to do. I googled the word 'Virago', asking for its meaning and origin. And this is what came up: The original Latin meaning of virago was **"female warrior"**. But in later centuries the meaning shifted toward the negative. The most famous virago in English literature is the ferocious Kate in Shakespeare's The Taming of the Shrew. I thought about that for a second or two, wondering if the new owner had changed the name as some kind of signal to us.

And that was about it for my day. I rang Pamela

quickly and told her I'd be home soon and then toddled down to the car park where I got the attendant on duty to ring for a taxi as I'd left the car at home that morning. It took me straight back to the flat and, once there, I had a nice dinner and finally collapsed into bed where I slept like a baby, thinking that I had done all I could for the moment.

CHAPTER 9

SATURDAY AM

I didn't bother going into work myself until shortly after 8 the next morning but, when I did get in, I found an urgent message from Sir M to get in touch 'at my earliest convenience' which meant right now in his parlance. So I went upstairs to his office where I found him still deluged by all my paperwork.

'I spoke to the PM yesterday and he nearly went ballistic when he heard about your Russian connection,' he said without preamble. 'Needless to say, he asked for proof and I said we didn't have any yet, just very strong suspicions. He also asked about the ship and I told him the name and the fact that, although we had no incontrovertible proof, the evidence against it was mounting up all the time. I think it's time to get that proof, don't you, Jack?' There he paused and looked at me with a steely gaze. 'I suggest one of the first things you need to know is more about cable laying ships and I asked the PM if he could find us a top expert on them who could have a look at those photos of yours and he said he'd get onto it straight after talking to the American

President and he's just got back to me on that. It seems that we only have a couple of people here in the UK who know much about them and they're both based up in Aberdeen. I've got their names, phone numbers and addresses here.' And now he passed me a slip of paper. He also said, incidentally that, provided we can get some proof of these allegations, the whole weight of the USA would be put behind our enquiries.' He stopped there and I knew it was my turn to speak.

'Thanks very much, Sir, for this,' I said, waving the piece of paper at him. 'You're right of course. We do need more concrete proof and I'm sorry I didn't think of this myself. I've been too busy looking at the nuts and bolts of the operation rather than seeing the bigger picture.' I didn't bother mentioning to him that I'd already tasked Alan and Lucy with finding out as much as possible about the ship. He seemed mollified by my words and waved me out after making another snide comment about the mountains of paper he was surrounded by. I returned pensively to my own office, thinking how I'd just assumed that everyone else would be swept along by my enthusiasm and forgetting that we did indeed need concrete proof if we were to be believed. However, it was certainly all to the good that I had a backstop like Sir M to remind me.

So, as soon as I got back to the office, I at once rang the two numbers and managed to catch one of the guys at home. His name was Sean Stephenson and he had an attractive Edinburgh burr. I introduced myself and asked him if he'd like an all-expenses paid trip to London in the service of his country. He sounded rather gob-smacked to being telephoned by MI5 but almost immediately agreed after saying he'd have to re-arrange a couple of things. I asked him if he could fly down today and he said yes, that shouldn't be a problem, adding that it was a good thing it was Saturday. 'Take a taxi to MI5 headquarters and someone will meet you at reception,' I said.

'Can you tell me what this is all about?'

'No. I'm afraid not over the phone but you will of course be briefed when you get here.'

'OK. I should be able to get to you around lunch time.'

'That would be brilliant if you could. We're all under rather a lot of pressure here.' And he said he presumed that was the normal state of affairs with a job like mine. I grimaced down the line but agreed with him and we both hung up. Good. At least that's sorted, I thought to myself.

I looked at my watch and was surprised to see it was nearly 9am already. So I went to the conference room where the others were slowly drifting in. When we were all assembled, I asked if anybody had had any more thoughts on their tasks. And Alan spoke up.

'Lucy and I reckon it might be better if one of us went up to Liverpool to see if anybody there can remember anything about the Virago. We reckon something like this would be better done face-to-face rather than over the phone.'

'Absolutely. Why didn't I think of that? Why don't you go, Alan? Fly if it's faster. Take as long as you need. No offence, Lucy, but Alan has the seniority and might be inclined to be taken a little more seriously. But you'll still have plenty to be getting on with here. If you need help, Lucy, just call on one of the others and I'm sure they'll willingly give you a hand. I think your task should take priority over finding the mastermind.'

'Yes, boss,' she said.

'Now, what have I been up to?' And I proceeded to give them a rundown on my meeting this morning with Sir M and how he's said that if we could get proof positive of my suspicions, the Americans would back us all the way. Then I told them about his suggestion which I'd followed through on and how a top expert on cable laying ships was expected here by about lunchtime. He was flying down from Aberdeen, I said, and I hoped that he would be able to give us the proof we needed that there was, indeed, something fishy about the ship. Finally I asked everyone to collect the photos from the walls of the conference room, which was quickly done, and, after I'd stowed them away safely in my briefcase, I wished them all good hunting and told them we'd meet up again at 5pm. Then it was back to my own office where I spent the rest of the morning ringing Toby and Sir M and bringing them up to speed and typing up my notes on the case so far. I just hoped I wasn't about to drop any of the balls I was trying to juggle.

CHAPTER 10

SATURDAY PM

When 1 o'clock came and went with no sign of Mr Stephenson, I began to worry if he'd been delayed. My stomach was beginning to growl and I knew I'd have to eat soon but then, about half an hour later, I got the message I'd been waiting for that someone was here to see me. I went straight down to the ground floor and met Mr Stephenson (call me Sean, please) and I asked him if he'd been delayed. He said he'd had to wait over an hour at Aberdeen airport for the incoming flight which brought him down to London and I thanked him again for coming at such short notice. Then I took him up to the executive dining room where we had a decent lunch and I told him that I was afraid he'd have to sign the Official Secrets Act before I could start to brief him. He said he presumed it was something to do with cable laying ships as that was the only thing he really knew much about and I had to shush him. Actually I liked him. He seemed like a decent cove.

Then it was back to my office where he signed the Act without demur and at last I was ready to show him the photographs. He looked through them all carefully, asking for a magnifying glass which I promptly gave him. I hadn't told him why he was looking at them, not wanting to prejudice him, and also because he wasn't cleared for that information.

'So, comments?' I said when he'd finished, turning on the tape recorder in my pocket and feeling a little guilty about doing so. But I wanted an exact record of everything he said.

'To most outward appearances, it appears to be a perfectly normal cable laying ship,' he said slowly 'but there are several things that bother me, not least the large structure on the foredeck which I've never seen before on one of these ships. Also there's the colour of it. I've never seen one before painted battleship grey. Usually they are red or red and white. It's almost as if it's been camouflaged. Then there's also the aerial display which is rather excessive for one of them. But the strangest thing of all for me is the submersible which appears to be completely new and untouched by the sea. It looks like it's just been unwrapped from its packaging. I have seen these working and normally when they are raised, they tend to be festooned with sea detritus, weed and suchlike, and the crew never bother cleaning them since they always get a cleaning when they're put back in the water. When did it leave port?'

'About 8 weeks ago,' I replied.

'Plenty of time to deploy it then,' he mused. 'Oh yes, a couple of other things: I'm not at all sure what the crew are doing. It all looks rather staged to me, as if they're putting on a show for someone watching. And finally, I don't recognise the officer and I thought I knew all the officers on these ships working out of Britain. It's possible, I suppose, that he's been imported if the original guy got sick or something. But that's never happened in my experience. Part of my job is to go around the country and check them before they leave port. In fact, I checked on this ship before it left Liverpool.'

'Did you now? That is very interesting. How long before it left?'

'Oh, it must have been back in February some time. I'd need my diary to check the exact date.'

'And I presume none of these oddities were evident when you checked it?'

'Yes, that's right. I assume they must have been added later.'

'What about the name of the ship, Virago? Was it called that when you checked it?'

'Silly me. How could I forget such an important detail? No, it wasn't. I must have read it as The Vertigo, which it looks remarkably like, both the name and the ship, and just assumed it was the Vertigo. We're trained just to look at the lines of a ship which can normally tell us its name. But I suppose it could have changed its name after I'd OK'ed it for sailing, especially if it had a new owner.'

'Thanks very much. That's extremely helpful. Is there anything you'd like to add?'

'No, I don't think so.'

'Would you be prepared to write a sworn statement,

including everything you've mentioned to me, that I can show to my superiors?'

'Yes, sure. That shouldn't be a problem.'

'Thanks ever so much, Sean. If I leave you alone to write it, I wonder if you could just tell my secretary outside when you've finished and I'll come straight back and see you out, with a brief detour to Accounts, of course, for your expenses?' Here I paused and grinned at him and he grinned back before I continued, 'As I said earlier, you may just have done your country a great service.'

'Is that it? Don't I get any kind of explanation of what this is all about?'

'No, I'm afraid not. It's all top secret. It's just possible that you might read a story in the newspapers about it all but I wouldn't count on it.'

'Oh well. It was worth asking.'

'I would have done exactly the same in your position.' And there I left him with a normal statement form to fill in and went straight up to Sir M's. There I played him the entire tape, which fortunately had come out perfectly clear, and, when I'd finished, I asked him if that was proof enough that the Virago was a dodgy proposition.

He sat back in his chair and considered it. 'Yes, I think so,' he said finally. 'It should be enough for our political masters at least.'

I breathed a huge sigh of relief and then told him that I was going straight down to Lucy's office to see if Alan had been in touch with her and that I'd bring him the sworn statement as soon as Sean had finished it. 'OK,' he said. 'Go. But leave the tape with me in case we need it as backup.'

'Yes, Sir,' I said and then I was out of there and racing through the building to Lucy's small office. I burst in and said without preamble, 'Any news from Alan?'

'Yes. As a matter of fact, he just phoned to say he'd managed to get hold of the crew roster and he's e-mailing it through now,' she replied in her usual equable manner, apparently not phased at all by my sudden appearance.

'Good man. Can you ring him back and congratulate him from me and also tell him that I've got the proof we need that the ship is, indeed, very dodgy. So now we can really get things moving. Oh, and also tell him that, if he needs to spend the night in Liverpool, to go ahead and do so. I expect there are other documents he's looking for, not least a plan of the ship and a list of any changes to the vessel made since February.'

'Yes, sir. And well done yourself,' but I was already out of there and running back to my own office. I arrived slightly out of breath and at once asked Sean if he'd finished.

'Yes. Just done,' he said, passing me the official-looking form. I skimmed it to make sure he hadn't missed anything important but he seemed to have included all the points he'd made earlier.

'Perfect. Thanks very much again. Now we just need to get this notarised and then you'll be free to go. One moment while I ring one of our in-house lawyers.' This was quickly done and soon, after a quick trip to Accounts where I gave him his expenses money, we were down in reception where I asked the lady on the desk to get him a taxi. It came quickly and I saw him outside, reminding him of the Official Secrets Act he'd signed and how he couldn't talk to anyone about our conversation, not even a partner.

He grimaced and said, 'Understood. Loud and clear.' Then we shook hands and he disappeared in the direction of City Airport. I looked at my watch and saw it was 4pm already. 'Time to go back to Sir M,' I said to myself. So back I went upstairs, clutching my precious piece of paper, where I found him still trying to tackle my mountains of paperwork.

'Have you got it?' he asked and I presented it to him. He read it quickly and then said, 'I notice that he's put his ideas in order of importance, always a good thing to do with politicos whose attention span is often rather limited. OK. I think I'll take this straight round to Downing Street. Let's hope they can manage to convince the Americans finally of the importance of this.'

'Indeed, yes, Sir. Without them I don't think we've got a chance in Hades of stopping the plot in time. Can I have my tape back now? I'd like to play it for my team.' He passed it to me and I promptly left his office and went back to my own. I had some thinking to do and I only had about half an hour to do it in.

Then when 5 o'clock came round, I went back to the conference room where I found everyone already assembled and started by playing the tape for them. Then, after they'd had a chance to assimilate it, I told them that Sir M was probably already on his way to

Downing Street with the sworn statement and now we just had to leave everything up to the PM, reiterating the importance of getting the Americans on board. They all nodded in agreement and now I said, 'Have you guys got anything for me? I know Lucy has so perhaps she should start.'

She got up and handed round copies of the crew roster, saying, 'These come courtesy of Alan. I'm sure you'll notice the names.'

I skimmed the longish document and then gasped. It seemed like all the names were Arabic! Then Lucy said, 'After asking a lot of questions, Alan says that the reason given for them all being Arabic was that the ship had been bought by a consortium based in Abu Dhabi and that was where they were headed to lay some cables unless something else came up demanding that they change their plans.'

'Just about plausible,' I said, grudgingly admiring the foresight of the operation's planners. 'It seems to me that the next step should be finding out whether there were sound reasons for them going to the mid-Atlantic. But I think we'll need the Americans for that. Does anyone recognise any of the names?' But there were doleful shakes of the head around the table. 'Oh well, I never expected them to make it that easy for us. I expect that most of them are travelling on false passports. Lucy, can you get back to Alan and find out if there are any photos to go with the names, at least of the officers? That would certainly help us in identifying them if any of them are on our books.' She nodded, making a note in her file. 'OK.

Now have any of the rest of you made any progress with identifying the mastermind behind all this?'

Now Dennis spoke up. 'Possibly, sir. There is one name that keeps cropping up. Alexei Giorgiev. A low-level functionary in the Russian consulate – apparently. He came to Britain about 9 months ago and, again apparently, does very little actual work at the Consulate. A classic example of the typical Russian spy, I hear you say. But what brought him to our attention was first his age – he's 52, far too old to be just starting out – and secondly his life style which is extravagant, to put it mildly. He has a penthouse apartment in a chic block near Canary Wharf and appears to do a lot of travelling around the country where he mixes with all kinds of people, both rich and not-so-rich. So a suspicious-looking character, to say the least. How he's managed to stay off our radar so far, God only knows. Oh, and he speaks perfect English with very little trace of an accent.'

'Hmm. It sounds either like he's got a rich patron back in mother Russia or he's a self-made man trying to see a little of the wide, wicked world before he pops his clogs. Have you got a picture of the guy?'

Now Felicity stood up and proceeded to pass around a photo of the elusive Alexei. He appeared to be dressed in a very expensive suit and looked very distinguished with salt-and-pepper hair and a well-trimmed beard and moustache. The photo was probably taken surreptitiously as he had his head back and was laughing at something someone not in the picture was saying.

'He looks like a bloody oligarch himself – certainly not like a low-level functionary in the Consulate.'

'Yes, that's exactly what we thought,' Felicity said now.

'And your gut feeling is that this could be our man?'

'Yes, sir. I know we've never seen a Russian spy quite like this before but his appearance and obvious money would seem to be excellent camouflage for all kinds of nefarious doings.'

'OK, chaps. Nice work. And congratulations on getting so much information on him so quickly. I think that's good enough for me. Now we really need to go to town on the guy. I'd like to know everything about him, from the size of his shoes to the brand of toothpaste he uses. Especially where he goes and who he meets. And I think you are the very people to find out. Gloria and Ben, perhaps you two could start looking into the source of his wealth.' I looked at my watch and saw it was nearly 6 o'clock. 'Now I think you could all do with a decent night's sleep. We'll all meet here again at 9am tomorrow. I did warn you there wouldn't be much time for R & R on this operation. Please apologise from me to your respective partners for calling you in on a Sunday but explain there's a bit of a flap on. Lucy, one final thing: before you go, could you ring Alan and send him a copy of the photo and ask him to show it around in Liverpool very discreetly and try to find out if it rings any bells. Thanks.' And she nodded again, making another note.

We left it there and I went back to my office and rang Pamela, telling her that I'd be home soon. She said dinner would be on the table when I arrived. I told her I loved her and rang off. I didn't bother ringing Sir M as I presumed he would still be closeted with the PM and I knew he'd be in the next morning, hopefully with some good news for me about the Americans. Then it was just a question of driving home, having a lovely meal and crashing out completely after my long and dramatic day.

CHAPTER 11

SUNDAY AM

I got to the office just before 8.30 myself and found a note from Sir M asking me to come up and see him so I went upstairs and found him in quite a good mood for a change, even if still surrounded by a number of my files.

'Hello, Jack. I was wondering when you'd condescend to honour us with your presence. Anyway, I've got good news for you. We've got the Americans on board at last and all gung-ho for action after I'd managed to convince the PM, who spent quite a long time on the phone with the President yesterday afternoon. I was there for the whole thing as he said he might need my help so I heard everything.'

'That is good news indeed, Sir,' I said. 'I've been thinking about how they could help and decided that the first thing we need is satellite coverage of the ship on a 24/7 basis until this whole thing is resolved. Then also I think we need one of their navy ships on standby not too far away, preferably one which has anti-ballistic missile capability in case the whole thing should go pear-shaped. If they could put a mini-stealth sub on board, that would be brilliant, as I like the idea of mining the ship as a threat of last resort. Also it might be very useful to have the use of one of their ocean-going coast guard vessels since I also like Alan's idea of accusing them of drug or gun running and asking whether the ship could be searched. '

'Hmm. Not asking for much, are you?' he said now, busy making notes.

'Not really, Sir, no, not if you consider the seriousness of the possible outcome.'

'OK. I agree. I'll get back to the PM with the list of your requests and we'll see what transpires.'

'Thanks a lot, Sir. Stress the time factor, please. Now, Sir, there is another matter I need to bring to your attention. My team think they've identified a Russian as the possible mastermind behind all this. A certain Alexei Georgiev. They seem fairly certain.' And I proceeded to tell him why they were so suspicious of him and what I had asked them to do. He grunted with approval when I'd finished and said, 'OK. Well, you've certainly got the right people to watch him.'

'That's almost exactly what I said, Sir. I reckoned it would give them some good practice even if it turned out to be a bummer.'

'OK. Well, Jack. Go and do your thing and I'll go and do mine. I'll mention your Alexei to the PM as I presume you'll be doing to Toby.' And on that note I left him.

By then it was nearly time to go back to the conference room. But, before I did, I decided to call Toby as I wanted to ask him about 'my Alexei'. He picked up at once on his mobile and I told him first about the Americans coming on board and he whistled with relief, saying 'Well done, Jack. How did you manage to accomplish that so quickly?' And I reminded him of the cable laying ship guy I'd met yesterday and how he'd come up trumps. I told him I'd send him a copy of his sworn testimony and he said, 'Thanks a lot.' Then I asked him about Alexei, saying that he was my team's number one suspect as the mastermind and whether he could get me any more information about him from Russia as I didn't want my team barking up completely the wrong tree. 'Sure, I'll do some digging. No peace for the wicked, eh?' he said before we said goodbye.

When I got to the conference room, I was delighted to see Alan there, carrying a big bundle of documents, so we were all present and correct again. 'I thought I'd better come back for this meeting. I can always return to Liverpool again, if needed.' I approved of his thinking and said so.

Then we got down to business which consisted of me starting by telling them what Sir M had told me that morning, to which they all clapped, and what I had said in return. 'Anything I forgot?' I finished and there were multiple shakes of the head around the table, Felicity speaking for all of them saying, 'No, we reckon you've covered all the bases you can, for the present at least.'

'Thanks, guys,' I said. After that I asked Alan what he'd brought back from Liverpool with him and he opened his bundle of documents and handed copies of everything around. First, there was a plan of the ship, named Vertigo then, showing the basic deck plans including the crew quarters.

'This could be very useful if we have to storm the ship,' I mused.

'My thoughts too, sir,' he said.

Then he continued, 'I'm afraid the harbour authority doesn't keep photos of the crew, sir. They told me that you'd have to apply to the new owners for them.'

'Pity,' I said. 'Anything else you've got up your sleeve, Alan?'

'Yes. The second document you've got shows the modifications to the vessel which were carried out in March this year.' I looked at it carefully and at once noticed the structure on the foredeck. It looked like just an empty space, lined with metal, maybe steel, with a large kind of, apparently, electronically-controlled door in the top. The plans showed a lift from it going down to the hold.

'Did they say what this was for?' I asked, pointing at what I meant.

'They said they didn't know themselves. Just that it was on the instructions of the new owners. But presumably it's for lifting something heavy out of the hold.'

'Like a missile,' I said grimly.

'Exactly, sir. And the last piece of news is about Alexei. I showed the photo to the head honcho of the restoration work, down at the pub actually, and he immediately recognised him as the officially- credited representative of the Abu Dhabi consortium who visited only once when the work was finished and signed it off. And that's the sum total of what I discovered.'

'That's brilliant, Alan. It's more than I reckoned you'd be able to do, especially so quickly,' I said and he preened a little in pleasure. 'Now we certainly have some sort of confirmation of Alexei being mixed up in all this. So now it's even more important to discover all we can about him. I've already asked Toby to find out what he can from his Russian contacts.' The rest of the meeting was taken up with organising who was going to do what about Alexei. 'Let's meet back here at 6. Don't worry if you can't make it. Just keep Alan apprised of where you are and any progress you've made. Remember, guys,' I concluded. 'You'll have to be *very* discreet,' and they all nodded. I didn't include Gloria or Ben as they were already tasked with looking into the source of his money and I sent Alan off home to sleep as I knew that he must have been up most of the night working or travelling.

'Thank you, sir,' he said. 'It's true I am a bit tired and would very much appreciate seeing my family.'

'Thank *you*, Alan, for a very successful mission,' I said. 'Oh yes, there is one other thing before I forget. Did you find out the name of the consortium?'

'Sorry, sir. I forgot to tell you. It is called the Mustafa Ben-Ali consortium.'

'Thanks for that. I wonder if you, Ben, could do some digging around to find out what you can about it and leave Gloria with the job of tracing Alexei's money. Just what's publicly available to start with.'

'Sure, sir,' he replied, pleased, I think, to be given his

own job to do, and there we left it and they all went their separate ways.

I was desperate now to see how Sir M had got on with the PM / Americans but knew there was still one more thing I had to do before that. So I ran back to my office and from there e-mailed Toby with a copy of Sean's sworn statement and also the picture of Alexei which I figured might be useful in identifying him. After that it was back up to Sir M's office where I barged in and accosted him with the obvious question 'Have you got any news for me, Sir?'

He grinned like the proverbial Cheshire cat and said, 'Actually, yes, I do. It seems you've got yourself the use of an aircraft carrier.'

'What?! You've got to be kidding, Sir!'

'No, I'm not. Apparently, there's one about to leave Hyannis Port for a tour of the Mediterranean which is going to be diverted for your use. According to their navy chaps, they are the only ships in the fleet which carry an anti-ballistic missile system. In addition to that, they're prepared to supply you with a coastguard vessel but they said no, I'm afraid, to a mini stealth sub. Apparently they are still being tested for sea worthiness. Also they are now watching the Virago 24 / 7. So I hope, on the whole, you're a happy bunny.'

'Indeed, I am, Sir. It's more than I expected.'

'I told you, once the Americans pull their finger out, there's no stopping them. So everything seems to be going your way on this operation, eh, Jack? I'm just wondering when a wheel's going to fall off.'

'So am I, Sir, so am I, which reminds me, I've had yet more good news from Alan who's just arrived back from Liverpool.' And I proceeded to give him a rundown on everything he told us, showing him the plans of the ship with and without the modifications and finishing by mentioning Alexei's role in the plot so far.

'As far as these plans go, one thing strikes me at once. If this whole thing goes down to the wire, it seems to me that you'll only have one missile to deal with, not two, as, presumably, it'll take a while to bring the other up from the hold. Plenty of time, therefore, for your aircraft carrier to wipe the vessel off the face of the earth.'

'Yes, Sir. That's true. I hadn't thought of that,' I said, thinking what a bloodthirsty old bastard he could be when somebody dared to threaten his beloved country. 'Any comments about the Alexei connection?'

'No, not really but I will of course inform the PM. I presume you've got everything under control with that side of things.'

'I hope so, Sir. Oh, yes, there is one other very important thing. We need to find out as quickly as possible whether the cable needs repairing in the Virago's location. Can you please find someone, probably in the States, who could help us with that? I really should have done this earlier, I know.'

'Yes, I agree. That is very important and should give us the final verification that the bloody ship is up to no good. I'll ask the PM to get in touch with the Americans.'

'Thank you very much for that, Sir.' And that was pretty much the end of the meeting. So I went back to my office and continued to write up my notes on the case so far, not sure what else I could usefully be doing. As it was a Sunday, the office was very quiet with no distractions and I made good progress. I was working more or less on autopilot when I suddenly had a brainwave and immediately rang Sir M.

'Sir,' I said, 'I've had an idea. Do you think it might be possible for me to be airlifted out to the carrier and be there for the action, if there is any? I'm sure I could be of use and it is my operation after all.'

He harrumphed and thought for a bit. 'Yes, I don't see why not,' he said finally after what seemed like an interminable wait, although it was, in fact, only a few seconds. 'Let me speak to my old pal in the American navy who's actually rather high up now and has the ear of the President.'

'Thank you, Sir,' I breathed gratefully, punching the air with delight. I hung up, thinking about how many birds that would kill with one stone. It would get me out of the office and into the action, two of my main complaints about my present job. I might even be able to get my hands dirty! Also, on top of these two major considerations, I had never set foot on an American aircraft carrier which I thought might be an adventure in itself. I knew Pamela wouldn't be pleased if I was away for any length of time but a few days surely wouldn't hurt, would it? Now I could only wait. And soon it was lunchtime so I went on up to the executive canteen where I ate decently as usual but in a fever of impatience for my boss to get back to me.

CHAPTER 12

SUNDAY PM

He finally rang me about 2 pm and asked me to come and visit him so on up I went again. When I went in, he said, 'Well, Jack, I've heard back from my friend in the American navy who has spoken to the President. He said they would be delighted to have you on board and would be prepared to hand over all dealings with the terrorists to you since it *is* your case as you pointed out and you probably have more experience dealing with people like these than any of their own FBI experts. To be perfectly honest, I'm quite jealous as I'd love a short spell at sea again. You'll leave in a day or so from Lakenheath as soon as transport is arranged so I suggest you pack a bag. Oh, and don't forget to tell Pamela as little as possible,' he concluded with a twinkle in his eye.

'That is fantastic, Sir. Thanks ever so much for organising everything,' I enthused gratefully.

'That's OK,' he finished, 'but don't forget to be careful. Not too much of your derring-do's. We'd like you back here in one piece.'

'Oh, I won't, Sir, I promise.' And I left his office on a real high.

Then it was just a matter of ringing Toby to tell him about my upcoming trip on the American carrier. He whistled when I told him, saying, 'You lucky dog!' and I said that that was almost exactly what Sir M had said. He told me that MI6 hadn't managed to find any dirt on Alexei yet, except that he seemed to be travelling on a false passport but this wasn't very unusual for Russian diplomats. His real name was, apparently, Petrov Kandinsky, he said. There were, however, a couple of long, unexplained gaps in his CV which didn't bode well for his probity. 'But we'll get there in the end. I'll e-mail you with what we've got,' he finished and I thanked him and hung up. Now I knew it was down to my own team to find out what they could about the mysterious Alexei / Petrov.

I got a lot done by the time 6 o'clock came round and it was time to return to the conference room, armed with the information Toby had sent me. I found Alan there sitting in solitary splendour, looking much perkier than he had that morning. 'Don't worry, sir. They'll be along soon,' he said, 'except for Dennis and Lucy who are still out watching our man.' And that was Gloria's cue to come in, looking rather glum, I thought, closely followed by the others.

I'd already decided to let them go first so I began by asking Ben what, if anything, he'd found out about the consortium that bought the ship and modified it. 'Not a lot, sir,' he said, 'and that worries me. I found the names of the directors of the company and they all seem to be reasonably legal, if corrupt, but that is normal for that part of the world. The CEO of the company has the same name as the consortium, so I guess he's the top man, but I could find out very little about him, I'm afraid.' And there he stopped.

'Well, never mind. It's all grist to the mill,' I said. 'How about you, Gloria?'

'I seem to have hit a bit of a brick wall too,' she said. 'I did manage to access Alexei's private account which is in one of our high street banks but it's pretty innocuous. Just his daily living expenses which could be accounted for by his salary. He must have other accounts, maybe in other names. Sorry, sir.'

That reminded me. 'I may possibly be able to help you there. According to Toby, his real name's Petrov Kandinsky. He must be travelling on a false passport which, according to Toby again, is not that unusual for Russian diplomats working as spies. You could certainly try that.'

'Thank you, sir. I'll certainly do that,' she said, making a note.

'And what about the rest of you?' I asked now.

Felicity spoke up now. 'We've been keeping a close watch on him but the only times he left his flat were to go to a supermarket where he stocked up on essentials and to go out for a drink in one of his locals at lunchtime when he didn't talk to anyone. We tried to access his flat when he was out but I'm afraid were defeated by the excessive amount of security he's surrounded himself with, too much even for Canary Wharf. Short of getting a warrant and a squad of heavies from the Met, we reckon it's probably going to be impossible to get inside.'

'Thank you, Felicity. More grist for the mill, I reckon, but I don't think we've got the proof we need yet for a warrant. I think he's probably a night owl so I hope you guys have the stamina to keep going a while longer. I presume Dennis and Lucy will need relieving soon? Anything from them, Alan?'

'Let me check, sir.' And he looked at his mobile. 'Yes, sir. It seems that he left his flat a few minutes ago in a taxi and headed off in the direction of the West End. They are in hot pursuit.'

'Good. Well, now for my news. It looks like I'm going to sea, maybe even tomorrow. The Americans have loaned us a warship to investigate the Virago and have put me in charge of any negotiations there might be with the crew. I'm not sure how long I'll be away but it'll probably be a few days. So I'll be leaving you all in Alan's hands. OK?' I deliberately left it short and simple. I continued, 'Oh, and the other thing that's happening is that we should be hearing soon whether the Virago is actually doing any real work where she is, something I should have done much earlier. I'll leave you now to get on with any tasks you've been allocated but I hope you'll keep Alan updated. Any questions?' But there were none.

'Yes, boss,' they chorused and drifted out, leaving me alone with Alan.

'Well, Alan, I hope you can hold the fort for me. I think it's important to keep after Alexei or Petrov or whatever his name is. If you think you can get a warrant to enter his flat, by all means do so. I suggest you use Sam Bullock to get in (*the Commander of the Met's Special Forces Division and a man I've trusted with my life on many occasions – see my previous memoirs*). And for God's sake, don't lose him. Perhaps you should alert the airports and ports now. I'd hate to see him swanning off back to Russia, ready to perpetrate more mischief. Remember I'll be leaving my mobile on all the time and if there's no signal, I'll make sure I get the Americans to give me a way to communicate with you. I expect to be kept updated on a daily basis.' And there I left it, not wanting to swamp him with too many orders.

He was busy taking notes and just said, 'Yes, boss.'

'Thanks, Alan. I'm off home now to tell my wife I have to go away and to pack a few things.'

'Good luck, sir.'

'Thanks. I hope I won't need it,' which signalled the end of another meeting. I looked at my watch and saw it was now approaching 7 o'clock. Not too late for dinner at home. I rang Pamela and told her to expect me in about three quarters of an hour, went down to the garage, got my car and drove carefully home, not wanting to have an accident at this stage of the proceedings but also rehearsing what I'd say to my wife.

I'd decided to keep it as simple as possible and said during dinner, 'I'm sorry, darling, but I'm afraid I have to go away for a few days for work.'

She knew of course that occasionally I had to go away

on business and just sighed and said, 'I hope it's nowhere too nice.'

'Actually, no, it's not. And it's classified.'

'Every spy's excuse for keeping a mistress,' she said tartly which made me grin but I didn't respond except to say, 'Don't be ridiculous, darling. Can we go to bed now?' a suggestion which she responded to in a most positive fashion.

When I knew she was asleep, I got up and packed one of my large, battered trusty holdalls, remembering to put in some warm clothes as I assumed it would be chilly in the middle of the ocean. I laid my pistol on top and my laptop in one of the outside pockets and lifted it. Not too heavy, I thought. Good. Then I remembered one other thing: a bottle of decent whiskey and I stowed that away too. After that I just collapsed into bed and slept the rest of the night without being disturbed.

CHAPTER 13

MONDAY TO 6PM

I waited around all morning for the phone call telling me I was on my way but it didn't come. Only one thing happened of note: I had a call from Sir M to tell me that the Americans had got back to the PM to say that the ship couldn't be up to any good as there were no repairs or laying of cables scheduled for its neck of the woods. That was really a huge relief as I still hadn't been sure that the whole thing wasn't a red herring or a complete waste of time. Actually I was amazed that we had managed to make so much progress in such a short space of time – only 5 days. It usually took quite a bit longer to get where we were on important cases like this.

But then, at about 1.30 pm, I was just doing the washing up after lunch which I'd eaten alone since Pamela was out with some of her mates, when it came. A friendly American voice on my mobile saying, 'We're ready for you now, Mr Sanderson. So if you could make your way to Lakenheath, you'll find a plane waiting for you. Don't forget to bring your documentation. Otherwise you might find it difficult to access the base.'

'Thank you very much,' I said, 'and don't worry. I won't.' Then it was just a quick question of checking I had everything I'd need, leaving a note for Pamela, lugging my bag to the lift, heading down to the garage and I was away. It took me a couple of hours to get there, only being delayed for a short time getting out of London as it wasn't the rush hour. When I arrived, I had to go through the usual security rigmarole but this was soon very efficiently done and I was escorted by one of the guards to a hangar. He left me there, taking my luggage off the back seat and saying, 'don't worry, sir, we'll take care of your car,' and I went inside. I'd actually done something like this before (*see my memoir, The Dirty Bomb Affair*) so I wasn't that surprised by all the gleaming new technology on display but it was certainly still very impressive.

There I met a very pleasant Major who said, 'Welcome, Mr Sanderson. Your ride awaits but first we must get you suited up after you've used the bathroom.' So I went there first (rather meekly but I could see the point) and did my business. I vaguely remembered what getting suited up entailed and managed to do it without too many problems. I even managed to ask a question while I was doing it regarding the type of plane I'd be flying in and was told it would be one of their latest generation of VTOL fighters, based on an old British design. Then he took me to meet the pilot, a young chap called Dylan, who immediately asked me if I had any experience in a modern fighter. I told him yes, a few years ago I'd flown in one of their new Lightning F1 stealth fighters to America and back and he looked quite impressed.

'But you're still a civilian and I need to run over safety precautions with you.'

'That's fine by me. It was some time ago, like I said,' I told him. So he went over everything with me and, funnily, I still remembered most of it. It was relatively straightforward, his most important instruction being 'Don't touch any of the controls! There'll only be you and me in the bird,' and I promised I wouldn't. I asked where we'd be flying to and he was rather surprised by my question.

'Haven't they told you, sir?' he asked.

'All I know is we're meeting up with a carrier. I don't even know its name or if it's left port. My question really relates to if we're flying direct and landing on it.'

'Yes, that's right. And it's called the Ohio. It's one of the newest carriers we've got and it's where I'm based. I flew off it early this morning.' He said the third sentence with a good deal of pride, I noticed.

'And who is its commanding officer?'

'That would be Admiral Pearson.'

'OK. That's all the questions I've got at the moment.'

'If you're ready, we might as well go now then, sir.'

'Fine.' And with that short exchange he picked up my bag as if it weighed nothing at all and walked out of the hangar to a jet parked now on the runway with a few technicians scurrying around it. We boarded (if that's the right word) and the technicians made sure I was securely buckled in and hooked up to the intercom and the oxygen supply. I was sitting directly behind him, in the navigator's seat, I presumed, but could still see everything that was going on outside through the big window at the front.

The technicians withdrew giving thumbs up signs to Dylan and there were a couple more minutes of sitting there while he chattered to Ground Control. Then he started the engines and very soon we were roaring down the runway and into the air, turning west very quickly. Soon we were at cruising altitude and I felt it safe to ask another question. 'I thought you said this was a VTOL fighter. Why didn't we take off vertically?'

'It is but when there's a decent runway we prefer to take off normally. It's a question of fuel conservation. We'll be landing vertically, however.'

'OK. I'm looking forward to that. How long is the flight going to be?'

'Only about a couple of hours. We'll be going supersonic soon.'

'OK. I'll leave you to fly this bird then.' And I shut up and dozed for a bit.

The next thing that happened was when Dylan interrupted my snooze by saying, 'We're going supersonic now,' and very soon there was the same sharp jolt as we passed through the sound barrier which I remembered from my trip on the stealth fighter. We were now travelling over featureless ocean just visible through the thin cloud cover. I continued to doze when Dylan said 'I suggest you wake up now, sir. We're nearly there.'

I shook my head, having tried to rub my eyes but failing because of the helmet I was wearing to clear it of muzziness, and looked out of the window. There still seemed to be nothing to see but then I noticed a dot on the horizon and we decelerated rapidly, coming closer and closer to the dot which resolved itself into the biggest ship I had ever seen. Then, before I knew it, we were in vertical mode and descending quickly. I thought we might crash into it but at the last minute Dylan decelerated even more and we landed on its deck with barely a thump. I was most impressed by Dylan's flying skill and told him so but he just said, 'It's what we're trained for, sir. Welcome to the Ohio.'

The next thing I knew we were surrounded by technicians again who opened the canopy and unbuckled me, disconnecting everything. Then I was out of the plane and standing somewhat unsteadily on the deck. I think this was more due to my needing to get over the effects of the flight than it was to the rocking of the ship itself which seemed to be ploughing through the waves very steadily indeed. Then another Major I think from his epaulettes, took my bag out from where it had been stowed and said or rather shouted as Dylan still hadn't powered down the engines completely, 'The Admiral is waiting to see you, sir. If you'd like to follow me.'

'Can I have a bit of a wash first?' I asked, as I felt I now needed a pee quite urgently.

'Yes, of course, sir,' he said. 'I was going to take you to your cabin first anyway.'

So I followed him inside the ship through multiple corridors, which, incidentally, all seemed to be pleasantly carpeted and lit and made it feel a bit like a 4 star hotel. We finally arrived at a fairly anonymous door which he opened with a flourish and ushered me inside. I was gobsmacked. It was quite big with a sitting room and a desk on which he deposited my luggage and I could see a double bed through an open door and another door which presumably led into a bathroom, all of which made it seem even more like a 4 star hotel. 'Gosh!' I enthused like an over-excited schoolboy. 'This is far nicer than I expected!'

'You are a special guest, sir,' he said simply. 'If you'd like to get washed up now and unpack your things, I'll take you to the Admiral when you're ready. Please just dial 0 on the phone and I'll answer,' he finished, gesturing to a phone on the desk.

'Thank you very much indeed,' I said gratefully.

'My pleasure, sir,' he replied and left the room.

I did my business in the bathroom which seemed to have all the mod cons you could possibly expect and then unpacked quickly, putting my clothes away in a large wardrobe in the bedroom. I noticed there was even a safe inside it and I put my notes, laptop and pistol away inside but decided to take in a smaller shoulder bag the photos of the Virago I'd brought and its plans to show the Admiral. I looked at my watch and saw it was still only 7 pm. Amazing, I thought to myself. Then I dialled

0 on the phone like I'd been told and the Major's voice responded at once. 'I'll be with you in about ten minutes, sir,' he said so I decided to lie down on the bed, not to sleep but just to see what the mattress was like and I wasn't surprised to find it very comfortable.

CHAPTER 14

THE REST OF MONDAY

So there I was walking along to meet my first American Admiral. Is this almost the beginning of my big adventure that I so craved, I asked myself. We walked up a lot of steps until we reached an imposing set of double wooden doors. My Major knocked and went in without waiting for a response and I followed, straightening my tie – I was wearing my one decent suit which I'd been wearing since London and was by now pretty rumpled. There appeared to be nobody in the huge room at first but then a swivel chair behind a massive oak desk turned and a little man emerged from behind it, wearing what I guessed was an Admiral's uniform. He was only about 5' 8" tall, was black, had a beaky nose, a full head of silvery hair and radiated authority like only those long used to command could. 'Jack Sanderson, I presume?' he said gruffly and I agreed that that was indeed me and said 'Admiral Pearson, I presume?' in an attempt to be humorous but he laughed and said 'Yes.' We shook hands and he said, 'Boy, am I pleased to see you! Did you have a good flight and is Tom here looking after you?'

I answered, 'Yes, thank you, sir, to both questions. A very smooth flight and very comfortable accommodation,' feeling slightly overwhelmed by all this bonhomie but then remembering that most Americans are extremely welcoming.

'Good, good. I understand you were the one to alert our masters to our mutual problem?'

'Yes, I guess I was.'

'So you probably know much more about it than me?'

'I'm not sure what you've been told, sir.'

'Well, we'll go into everything in detail later but first I think dinner is called for, don't you? You must be starving.'

'It's true I am rather hungry,' I agreed, remembering I hadn't eaten since lunchtime in a different time zone.

'Well, you've arrived just in time for dinner. Follow me and you can meet some of my senior officers.'

'Perfect, sir.'

So we left his stateroom, went down a flight of stairs, along another corridor, and arrived at another set of wooden doors with a number of waiters all dressed in spotless white and fussing over a large number of chafing dishes laid out on trolleys outside. They all straightened up and saluted smartly when the Admiral approached and he saluted back before entering the room. I gasped. It was like going into a 5 star restaurant. Tables all laid out with gleaming silver cutlery, expensive-looking crockery and linen table napkins. There was no alcohol, I noticed, and I wondered if it was possible to get a drink on board although I could see the point of not allowing it.

But the Admiral didn't dally, going straight in and saying in a loud voice 'Ladies and gentlemen, pay attention, please. This is our special guest, Mr Jack Sanderson, all the way from England, who is responsible for diverting us on our voyage across the Atlantic.' Meanwhile the assembled officers (there must have been about 20 people in the room) had all stood up in deference to their commander and, after his little speech, they all bowed to me. I felt a bit like a rock star. But then we all sat down with me on the Admiral's right, to a delicious fish starter.

'I hope you're not Vegan or anything like that. I believe there are lots of those now in your country,' the chap next to me said.

'Indeed not,' I replied with a mouthful of fish half way to my mouth. 'And yes, you're right. There are quite a few of them now.' But then he left me alone to eat and I devoured everything that was put on my plate. But all too soon the meal was finished and the Admiral called for silence again. 'Now to business, guys. Those of you who are involved, we'll meet in my quarters in 20 minutes.' And he stood up abruptly and left the room, calling over his shoulder, 'Follow me, Mr Sanderson.'

'Please call me Jack,' I said, trying to keep up with him. 'Nobody calls me Mr Sanderson.'

He turned when I said this and smiled. 'Sure, Jack. No problem,' he said. But we were soon at his quarters and he got busy arranging chairs. 'If you want to use the bathroom, Jack, it's through there.' And I followed his pointing finger into an even bigger bathroom than mine which actually had a proper bath tub in it rather than just a shower. I did my business and then washed my hands in the capacious sink, thinking I could get used to this life style.

When I came out, I found him sitting behind his desk again and he gestured to a chair in front of it so I sat down. 'Now, Jack, tell me a bit about yourself.' So I gave him a short, rather bowdlerised version of my life so far, not mentioning my alcohol dependency after my first wife died, which I was rather ashamed of, and he seemed satisfied. But then there was a knock on the door and six of his officers filed in, one of whom I noticed was a woman. 'These six are the only ones on the ship who have been fully apprised of our mission, as far as we understand it, since we have orders to keep it all absolutely top secret,' the Admiral began. 'Before you tell us your side of the story, perhaps we should tell you what *we* know.'

'That's a good idea,' I said.

And he proceeded to give me a succinct rundown on the problem as perceived by the Americans, starting with the letter sent to the President, how his advisors had convinced him it was a hoax and how he had decided to take it seriously only when the British PM had persuaded him because of the evidence we had collected, especially the fact that Russian money seemed to be behind the plot. This, apparently was what had galvanised him into action. Then he stopped, looked at me enquiringly and said, 'And now I have orders to do whatever you want about these wretched terrorists, which is rather unusual to put it mildly.'

'Fair enough, sir. Thank you for that. It puts me in the picture from your perspective. Now, what can I add to that?' I pulled out of my shoulder bag the photos of the Virago and said, 'These were taken last Friday by one of your own spy satellites and were what persuaded us to take the whole thing seriously. There are several anomalies about the ship, not least its colour, which makes it look almost like it's been deliberately camouflaged, the strange structure on the foredeck and all the aerials which, according to our own experts, are really not necessary.' There I paused to give them time to pore over the photos, the other officers all gathering around the Admiral's desk to look over his shoulder. Then I took the plans of the ship out of my bag also and spread them out, explaining that they had been acquired by one of my operatives just yesterday. 'Were they really?' I thought wonderingly to myself, and they were again studied with interest. I didn't bother about explaining Alexei's /Petrov's part in all this as I knew it wasn't relevant to their mission.

The Admiral then spoke up, 'I suppose the ultimate result you are hoping for is to foil these guys in their plot.' I nodded and he went on, 'And how exactly can we help?'

This was my cue to cut to the chase and I said, 'Well,' I said, 'first, I presume you have a company of Navy SEALS at your disposal.' And it was his turn to nod. 'Good. I'm hoping to negotiate with these maniacs, which

I've done before, but I don't hold out much hope there as, usually, the only thing they understand is violence. So I have to be able to threaten them and to make my threats come good if necessary. I've had plenty of time to think about this and, although it's a pity you don't have a mini stealth submarine on hand so that we could surreptitiously mine the ship and blow it up whenever we wanted, I have another idea now. I propose to take the SEALS out to the Virago in the Coast Guard cutter, which I presume you have hidden away somewhere on your ship.' And he nodded again. 'While we were having dinner I heard something about a big storm heading our way. Is this true?' And he nodded yet again. 'How long will it take to pass over?'

'About a couple of days,' he said, 'if our meteorological projections are correct.'

'That still leaves us enough time,' I said, thinking hard. 'Now, would it be possible, do you think, to drop a buoy in the sea not too far from the Virago, giving out a very short range distress signal from an imaginary yacht? I thought that might be a better reason to want to board the vessel than our original one of suspecting guns or drugs on board. Then, if they don't move, we'll have the final proof we need that it's definitely up to no good.' I knew of course that it was every ship's primary duty to go to the aid of a vessel in distress.

They all really perked up when I said this and I could see they were following my reasoning. The Admiral looked at one of his men and said now, 'How about it, Bradley? Is it feasible to do that?'

And Bradley, who was obviously a technical support officer of some sort, said, after thinking for a few seconds, 'Yes, I don't see why not. It breaks practically every maritime code in the book but, then, I suppose pointing nuclear weapons at us and threatening to detonate them if we don't pay a huge amount of money and release all our prisoners is even worse.'

'It's a clever idea, Jack, but what happens if they don't want to cooperate?' the Admiral said.

'That's a very good question, sir. And it brings me to the second part of my plan. I'd like to have a couple of your fighters in the air, ready to blow up the ship if necessary and also, as a last resort, your ABM system ready to destroy the missiles if they manage to launch them.' And there I stopped.

I could practically see the cogs turning in the Admiral's head and I waited with bated breath for his verdict on my plan. 'Well, Jack, if we're going to war, we might as well do it properly. So, yes, on the whole, I think your plan might work, although it might need to be refined somewhat. And now I understand why you needed a carrier.'

'Yes, sir. Thank you very much. Sorry I didn't mention that in my briefing,' I said with considerable relief. If he hadn't backed me, we would really have been up a gum tree although I didn't explain that, actually, a carrier was originally beyond my wildest dreams.

'Thanks for these,' he said, gesturing at all the pieces of paper littering his desk. 'I guess they could come in useful. Now, team, any ideas to improve on Jack's plan?'

'Yes, sir,' and it was the woman who spoke up now. 'Perhaps it might be possible while Jack's conferring with these madmen to send a couple of SEALS under the Virago to mine it.'

'Good idea, Sandra. You'd need to speak to them first to find out how long it's going to take,' the Admiral said. 'Anything else, guys?' But nobody had anything else to offer so they were all dismissed with orders to ruminate on what they'd heard and see if they could come up with improvements to my plan while Bradley was told to get on with designing the buoy, leaving me alone with the Admiral.

'So, Jack, anything else we can do for you?' he said.

'Yes, sir. There is, actually. I need a secure phone line to speak to my team at home, preferably on my mobile phone.'

'Oh, that's easily done. If you'd like to lend me your phone and tell me your number, I'll get one of my tech whizzes to sort it out in no time. I'll ask Tom to bring it back to you as soon as it's done. It shouldn't take more than a few minutes. Whenever we have to entertain important guests, they always ask for the same thing.'

'Thank you very much indeed, sir,' I said now, pulling it out of my pocket and giving him the number as I passed it to him. And that was almost the end of my very busy day. Tom appeared like a genie out of a bottle now and escorted me back to my room with instructions to see to my phone. I lay down on my bed fully clothed, shattered now, and was almost asleep when Tom reappeared with my phone, announcing, 'All done!' and I thanked him and, as soon as he left, rang Pamela, told her quickly that everything was fine and rang off before she had time to ask any questions. Then I rang Alan and asked if he had any news and he said that, so far, Alexei seemed to be behaving himself although he did visit a high-class brothel in Soho the previous evening which the team didn't have a hope of entering so God knew what he'd got up to in there. He hoped it was just a piece of nookey but he couldn't be sure. In addition, he said that Gloria was making slow progress in tracking down the source of his wealth but had nothing concrete yet. Then he asked how I was getting on and I told him that so far everything was hunky-dory and the Admiral was playing ball but that I had no idea how everything was going to turn out. I just hoped I'd covered all the bases. He wished me luck and rang off. And. finally, I could go to sleep properly so I undressed, did my evening ablutions and collapsed again into bed, remembering something I needed to ask the Admiral the next morning and that I needed to update Sir M just before I fell asleep, lulled by the soft sound of the engines.

CHAPTER 15

TUESDAY APPROX
7 AM – 11 AM

I slept well considering and got up and looked at my watch. It was already 10 am I noticed but then I remembered that we were a few hours behind England and relaxed. That was important – to find out the time here. I did all my usual morning stuff and dressed in comfortable clothes, including my old bomber jacket, before ringing Tom. He appeared promptly and I immediately asked him what time it was. 'It's 7.28,' he told me after consulting his watch and I adjusted my own.

'Would you like some breakfast now?' he asked.

'That would be lovely,' I said.

'Just dial 2 on your phone, ask for whatever you fancy and it will be delivered here.'

'Brilliant!' I said enthusiastically. 'Thanks, Tom.'

'My pleasure, sir. If you need me after you've finished, you know how to contact me.'

'I do need to see the Admiral again,' I told him.

'No problem, sir.' And he left.

So I dialled 2 and a cheerful American voice asked me what he could do for me and I ordered the kind of decent breakfast I usually only had when I went to a nice hotel in England. 'Do you want your eggs sunny side up or over easy?' he asked and I had to think for a moment before I answered. In my defence it was a while since I'd been to the States. 'Sunny side up,' I said.

'Coming right up,' he said.

I thought I could usefully call Sir M while I was waiting, knowing that he'd probably be in the office already so I did that.

'So you've got your communications sorted out,' was the first thing he said when he picked up.

'Yes, Sir.' And I proceeded to give him a proper rundown of my plans for the Virago, which I hadn't bothered to do with Alan the evening before.

'So it sounds like everything's still going your way,' he said when I'd finished.

'Seems to be, Sir,' I replied.

'Just don't get too cocky, young Jack,' he warned before hanging up. I wondered if he knew something I didn't but then decided he was just worrying about me in the hands of the Americans. I suspected he still hankered for the good old days before the war of Independence when the USA was still, mostly, a part of Britain.

I'd just hung up when there was a discreet knock on the door and, when I opened it, there was a young man outside with my breakfast which smelled heavenly. I ate heartily and finished quickly before ringing Tom again.

'I'm ready to be collected now,' I said and he replied, 'I'm on my way, sir.'

He turned up a few minutes later and we went back up to the Admiral's quarters where we found him signing lots of documents. 'Be with you shortly, Jack,' he said and I plonked myself down on the easy chair in front of his desk. He did, indeed, finish his signing quite quickly and he looked at me and enquired what he could do for me. I told him that I'd very much like to see where we were now and he said, 'A reasonable question. Why don't you follow me up to the bridge and I'll show you?'

He left his rooms and I followed him obediently, taking a lift I hadn't noticed just outside. We went up a number of floors and emerged into a huge room which reminded me somewhat of the bridge on the star ship Enterprise, right down to the massive plate glass window looking out over the ocean. It was full of computers and men and women all intently watching their screens and talking into microphones attached to their lapels. He took me over to a huge screen on the wall and showed me the dot which was us progressing steadily east in relation to the Virago which was represented by another dot on the screen. Next to it there was another much smaller screen with satellite imagery of the Virago projected onto it. Nothing much seemed to be happening on it except that I could see a few sailors who seemed to be battening down hatches, presumably in expectation of the coming storm. The submersible was still sitting on the deck and still looking as pristine as it had when I last saw it. I assumed now it was just for show, possibly because they hadn't been able to find any operators for it, which was a relief.

'Thank you very much, sir, for showing me that. Can you show me now where you intend to park the carrier?'

And he pointed to a spot in the ocean some way north east of the Virago, saying, 'We were told you wanted it parked out of sight and radar viewing of the Virago. This is probably the closest we can get to that.'

'And how long do you think it will take to reach there?' I asked now.

'About another 16 hours,' he said.

'And when will the storm hit?'

'It's already started actually. But we won't feel the full force until just before we arrive at our destination.'

'So, if we aim to have Bradley's buoy in the water in about 20 hours, do you think that will work time-wise?'

'Yes, I don't see why not.'

'Perfect. That's the timeline I was hoping for. So I'm hoping to take the cutter out in about 36 hours. OK?'

'Yes. That sounds good. The worst of the storm should have passed over us by then,' he said.

'One more thing I'd like: to meet the leader of the SEALS team I'll be taking. I need to OK my plan with him.'

'Sure. I'll set it up through Sandra.'

'Thanks a lot, sir.' We'd been talking in low voices until now; presumably to keep the mission secret from those in the room not vetted highly enough even though nobody seemed to be paying us the slightest attention. They were all much too busy. But now I raised my voice a bit and said a little bashfully, 'There is one more thing, sir, but it's personal. I wondered if I could have a tour of the ship. I've never been on a ship this size before and I'd love to look round it.'

He laughed and said, 'I thought you'd never ask. It's what all my visitors ask almost as soon as they come aboard. Yes, of course you can. I'll set it up with Tom. He's a kind of professional tour guide.'

'Thanks ever so much, sir. I'm really looking forward to it.'

'Now I do need to go back to work. So if you'll excuse me...'

'Of course, sir. I'm sorry to have taken up so much of your time.'

I followed him back to his quarters where he rang for Tom who promptly arrived. 'Mr Sanderson would like a tour of the ship. Could you arrange that, please, Tom? Oh, and Tom, nowhere is off limits to him.'

'Yes, sir. That's no problem at all.'

I followed Tom outside and he immediately said, 'When would you like to start your tour, sir?'

I looked at my watch and saw it was already just past nine. 'How about in a couple of hours? I have some work to do first.'

'Sure thing, sir. I'll come by and pick you up at 11. Do you remember the way back to your room?'

'Yes, thanks. I'll find it.' And he disappeared back in the opposite direction to the one I was going.

Find it I did without going round in too many circles and once there I first rang Toby to update him on my progress. He listened carefully to everything I had to tell him and commented, 'So everything's still going your way, old chap. That's good. Now I guess you want to hear what I've found out. Alexei / Petrov is an old hand at spying. He started his career at the St Petersburg school of languages where he apparently excelled and was promptly snapped up by the KGB and put to work, mainly in designing operations against the West. He survived all the purges and is rumoured to be very highly connected in the Kremlin. Apparently, he rarely leaves Russia. It looks as if you've caught yourself a very big fish, Jack. If you need any help bringing him in, you only have to ask.'

'Wow! Thanks a lot, Toby. Have you told Alan? He'll be very happy for the team.'

'No, not yet. I've only just found out the details. And yes, it was very clever of your team to get onto him so quickly. A nice case of intuition paying off. He really is a very slippery customer.'

'OK. I need to speak to him right now, I think. Thanks again and keep in touch.' And I disconnected.

I rang Alan immediately and told him as exactly as I could remember what Toby had told me. He whistled when he heard the news and said, 'Well, the team will be pleased they haven't been wasting their time.'

'My thoughts exactly. And Toby also said that if you needed any help with bringing him in, you only had to ask.'

'That could be very helpful in fact. The team are getting quite tired now and I'm afraid they might make a mistake and be spotted although this news should give them some extra adrenalin. I'll certainly take him up on his offer.'

'One other thing I just thought of: Do you think you have the evidence now you need to get that warrant to search his flat?'

He thought for a moment and then said, 'That's a very good point. Yes, I think we do. But I'm still not sure how we'd get in without him spotting something amiss.'

'Maybe Sam Bullock has some ideas on that.'

'Yes. Another good point. I can but ask. Thanks for all that, Jack.'

'My pleasure. Now I have to ring Sir M,' and I hung up. So I did that and he was as amazed as I and Alan had been at Toby's news about Alexei. Then I told him what I had talked about with the Admiral earlier and he only had one question when I'd finished. 'So when do you think you might be back here?'

'I reckon in about a couple of days or a bit more if everything goes according to plan.'

'Which it probably won't,' he said pessimistically. But then he continued, 'I was thinking about picking up Mr bloody Kandinsky and keeping him on ice here before you return and letting you have first crack at him. You have rather a good reputation at cracking difficult customers, when you don't shoot them, that is.'

'That would be great, Sir!' I said. 'I think that's an excellent idea.'

'Thought you'd like it,' he said. 'OK. It will be done.' And he disconnected abruptly.

Now I could only leave the London end of things to the pros there and focus on my mission here. But first a bit of R & R, I thought. I looked at my watch again and saw it was already 10.15. I only had three quarters of an hour before Tom was due to collect me and I wondered how I could fill the time. Then I decided I might as well continue working on my notes and I had brought them more or less up to date when Tom knocked.

CHAPTER 16

THE REST OF TUESDAY

'Where do you want to go first?' he enquired amiably.

'Just take me on your normal tourist tour, Tom. At least it'll give me an idea of the layout of the ship. When we finish, I'll tell you if there's anything else I want to see. Remember I've already seen the bridge.'

'Very well, sir. Follow me.' He took me down in another, much bigger lift this time to the hangar deck where hundreds, seemingly, of gleaming airplanes were being checked by numerous technicians. It was an enormous space, positively cavernous, about the size of four football pitches I calculated, and there were many different kinds of plane on view, from giant Sikorsky helicopters to the matt black stealth fighters I remembered so well. I was completely wowed. It was also very noisy and I had to shout to make myself heard. 'How do they get the planes up to the deck?' I asked. He beckoned to me to follow him and, after walking what seemed to be about half a mile, we came to a couple of huge lifts which took the planes up top. 'Can I go up to the deck, Tom? I'd like to feel the sea breeze on my face,' and I suddenly realised how true this was. I hadn't been outside since I stepped off the fighter and was starting to feel a bit claustrophobic. 'Yes, sure,' he said. And he took me around a corner to a much smaller lift which took us quickly up to the main deck. On the way (it was much quieter in the lift and I didn't have to shout) I said to him, 'Gosh! That was impressive!' and he laughed and said, 'That's exactly the reaction of all our visitors. Except that they don't usually say "Gosh!". It's usually much more profane.' And it was my turn to laugh.

Then we stepped outside and I was immediately buffeted by what felt like a Force 10 gale and I had to zip up my jacket. I also had to shout again to make myself heard. There was also the noise of jets taking off and landing in what appeared to be a continual procession and a strong smell of jet fuel. 'Is it always this busy?' I asked and he replied, 'No, actually it's not. I think it's probably because you're on board. We seem to be almost on a war footing.' That sobered me up and I thought 'All this for me?'

But then I noticed a flotilla of smaller warships following us and asked, pointing, 'What are those?'

'They're our escorts in case we meet any hostiles. We always have them with us.'

'Oh, yes. Of course,' I said, embarrassed by my ignorance. I'd completely forgotten that of course a carrier wouldn't travel all by itself in spite of its fearsome armoury. 'Do you have any submarines with you?' I asked now.

'That's above my pay grade, I'm afraid. But usually, yes. However, as this was meant to be just a friendly visit to some allies, I'm not sure.'

Another thing I hadn't known. 'Thanks, Tom. I think I've had enough sea breeze for a while.'

'Yes, sir. Don't forget there's a storm on the way. It's not always this windy.'

'No, I hadn't forgotten,' although in fact I had, temporarily at least. He led me back inside the ship to where it was much quieter and warmer. 'Well,' he said, 'you've seen probably the two most exciting things on the ship. I hope the rest of the tour won't be a letdown.'

'I'm sure it won't,' I replied. 'Remember I want to get the basic layout fixed in my mind. But, come to think of it, there are two things in particular I'd like to see: first, the coastguard cutter you've got on board and second, your anti ballistic missile system.'

'Yes, sir. We're actually much closer to the ABM's here. I'll take you there first if that's OK.'

'Yes, that's fine. Lead on, McDuff.' I followed him to the foredeck just below the bridge and he stopped outside a smallish steel door. I noticed a camera pointing at me.

'This is as far as I'm allowed to go, sir. It's all very top secret inside. I'll wait for you here.'

I thanked him and knocked on the door. It opened slowly and mechanically and one of the officers who'd been at the briefing came out. 'Mr Sanderson. Welcome. We were wondering when you'd stop by.' I went in thinking about the questions I needed to ask and was confronted by a cramped space with computer screens all around and four officers sitting in front of them. He was obviously the boss here as all the others stood up from behind the desks and saluted me and I noticed one empty desk near the door without a screen but with lots of papers on it which I reckoned must be his. 'Hello, guys, at ease,' I said. 'I've just got a few questions for you, the most important one being: What is your success rate in shooting down missiles?'

The boss replied for them all and said, 'Honestly, sir, it's not as good as we'd like. We succeed about 75% of the time but of course it helps to know exactly where they're located and in your case, we do.'

'And does it make any difference if they're ICBM's or medium range missiles?'

'We haven't had much practice with medium range missiles, to be honest, sir, since they're not perceived as big of a threat. But the success rate would seem to be about the same.'

'And I sincerely hope you won't need to practice when my mission is ongoing. You are only my last resort.'

'We know that, sir.'

And I went on to ask a few more technical questions about range, height of operation and speed of response and he answered them all as fully as he could. Finally I thanked him for his honesty and left the room in a thoughtful frame of mind.

I met up again with Tom who'd been waiting patiently outside in the cold and we went back into the main part of the ship which, in spite of its air conditioning, was still much warmer than it was outside.

'So, would you like to go to see your cutter now, sir, or would you rather have some lunch?' he asked.

I looked at my watch and saw it was 12.30 already as my stomach was reminding me so I said, 'I think lunch sounds good first. Where do you usually eat?'

'Us lowly officers have our own restaurant,' he said modestly.

'That sounds perfect. I found all the pomp and ceremony of dinner last night rather overwhelming.' So I followed him there and we had a very decent, hot meal to the curious stares of the officers present but weren't disturbed and, after we'd eaten, I said, 'I feel much revived now, Tom. I think I'm ready to see my cutter now.' So we went down many more corridors and into another lift which took us down into another largish kind of hangar where there were quite a few boats on display. I thought wryly to myself it'll take me weeks just to learn the basic layout of the ship.

But there was one boat which stood out. It was quite a bit larger than any of the others, having at least two decks I could see and with US Coastguard newly painted on the side. 'I suppose that's it,' I said, heading straight for it. I noticed it also had a heavy machine gun on the foredeck which I thought could come in very handy. There were a number of hard-bitten-looking types working on it and I wondered if any of them were my SEALS. They certainly reminded me very strongly of the Royal Marine Commandos I'd had dealings with in England once (*see my memoir The Drone Attack*). One of them came forward and held out his hand, 'I'm Captain Chuck Kelly and I'd guess you are Jack Sanderson.' I said I was and he said, 'I'll be leading your team of SEALS,' shaking my hand firmly. So I was right, glad that my intuition hadn't let me down.

'I'm very pleased to meet you,' I said. 'I was hoping to today.'

'I know. Sandra told me. But this is fortuitous.'

'I agree,' I said, liking him already. 'Is there somewhere we could talk privately?' I didn't want to have to shout over the noise of all the banging and hammering going on in the hangar.

'Yes, sure. Why don't we go back to my quarters?'

'Good thinking,' I said. Then I turned to Tom and said, 'Thanks very much for the tour, Tom, but I don't think I'll need you for the rest of the day. I'm sure someone can show me back to my cabin.'

'OK, sir. You know how to get in touch if you need me.' And saluting smartly, he left.

Chuck yelled at his men, 'Guys, this is Jack Sanderson. He's the one who's hi-jacked the ship and who will be in charge of our little mission. Remember his face.' His men stopped what they were doing, grinning and saluting me. Then he yelled, 'Keep at it, guys. I'll be back soon.'

'Is that a threat or a promise, sir?' one of them yelled back and I recognised the camaraderie of a group who obviously knew each very well and functioned well together as a unit. But Chuck ignored the banter and I was soon following him down yet more corridors I'd never seen before until I reached another anonymous door which he opened with his key and we both went inside. I was now in a comfortable but much smaller cabin than mine.

'OK. We can talk in here,' he said, plonking himself down on one of the hard, upright chairs flanking a desk and gesturing at the other.

I sat myself down and didn't waste time. 'What have you been told about the mission?' I said.

'Everything I need to know,' he replied. 'We're there to take out a boatload of hardened terrorists, if we're needed, on a cable- laying vessel called the Virago.'

'Yes. Very succinctly put. However, I think it's only fair to put you in the picture a little more. There are probably a couple of nuclear missiles on board aimed at your country and mine which could cause untold devastation if released.' I didn't pussyfoot around as I thought he wouldn't appreciate it.

The colour drained from his face and he replied slowly, 'Thanks for telling me. That does rather put a different complexion on what we have to do. I hope you haven't got any more shocks up your sleeve for me.'

I smiled at him and said, 'No, that's it. I do, however, have a number of questions for you.' And here I paused for a moment, marshalling my thoughts. 'First, how many of your guys are we taking?'

'I thought ten of us should be enough,' he said 'but now I'm not so sure. I hope you're not going to ask us to disarm the missiles.'

'No, certainly not. You know you'll be heavily outnumbered. The crew roster says there are 58 men on it. What happens if they're all armed?'

'We've faced worse odds than that before and survived,' he replied confidently and I believed him, 'and, anyway, we won't be outgunned. I've seen to that. We've been fighting rag heads for years.'

'Oh, so you know who you'll be up against?'

'A bunch of Arabs would be my guess.'

'Yes, you're absolutely right. I'm glad you're so confident,' I said hesitantly.

'Confident, yes, but complacent, no.'

And that was when I knew I could rely on him 100%. 'Good man!' I said now. 'OK. Let's move on. Is it going to be possible for you to mine the ship while I'm trying to talk to them?'

'It all depends how long you can give us. Ten minutes should be enough.'

'Good,' I said, 'That shouldn't be a problem, hopefully. And that reminds me of something else: Will you have someone on board who can speak Arabic and act as my interpreter if needed?'

'Yes, I have a couple of guys who speak fluent Arabic; one of them is actually of Arab extraction.'

'That's brilliant!' I enthused. 'Let's move on to the nuts and bolts of the operation now, shall we?' He nodded and I continued by quizzing him on the comms equipment they would need, stressing the need for reliable equipment not only between themselves but also between the cutter and the fighters which would be circling overhead and, most importantly, the ABM guys on the carrier.

'Our own equipment is tried and tested,' he said, 'but I didn't know we'd have fighter support or need the ABM guys on the carrier. But I'm sure it can be easily sorted out,' he said, making a note on a pad on his desk. 'It's good to hear we'll have fighter support if we need it and I'm glad you seem to have covered all the bases.'

'Thanks a lot, Chuck. And I'm glad we seem to be singing from the same song sheet. Were you given the plans of the Virago, by the way?'

'Yes, thanks. They could certainly come in handy if we have to storm the ship. I've left them with my men to study.'

'Good. Now it's just a matter of when we actually leave, I think.'

'Sandra told me that you were thinking of leaving about 2100 hours tomorrow night. Is this still true?' I realised then that the Admiral must have passed on my projected itinerary to Sandra, which pleased me.

'I thought that might work time-wise. The buoy should have had plenty of time to work by then.'

'Oh, yes. I heard about the buoy. Clever idea that. Yes, I don't see why not. If there are any delays, I'll let you know.'

'Thanks very much, Chuck. Well, I think that concludes our business.'

'Yes, I'm very glad we've had the chance for this chat. Do you want me to tell the guys about the nuclear weapons angle?'

'So am I, Chuck. So am I. And yes, I don't see why not. I think they deserve to know, don't you? But I'll leave it up to you.'

'OK. Thanks, Jack. Now I need to go and sort out the communications angle.'

'I just have one more simple question, Chuck. What were your guys doing to the cutter?'

'Primarily making sure it is 100% seaworthy. But some of them were also making storage space for our own armoury. We don't want to have our weapons to be flying all over the place if it gets rough out there.'

'I agree. Well, I think that's it. Thanks again.'

And after a few more pleasantries we parted company outside his quarters and I went on my way to find my own.

I found my own way back after only having to ask twice which I thought wasn't too bad considering the size of the ship and when I arrived, opening the door with the key Tom had given me, immediately phoned Tom to tell him that I needed a quiet night in and to let the Admiral know but that I'd see him, Tom, in the morning. He said, 'Of course, sir,' in his usual amiable way and I hung up. I looked at my watch and saw it was 4.15 already.

There was only one important phone call I wanted to make now to ask Sir M if they'd got Alexei so I did that. When he answered, he said, 'Yes, of course, Jack. I told you it would be done and it was. We've got him stewing nicely downstairs in the basement where he keeps on bleating about diplomatic immunity but, needless to say, is getting nowhere.'

'Well done, Sir. Please congratulate Alan for me. I'm really looking forward to speaking to him.' That was the essence of the conversation. Then I called Pamela and spent a few more minutes on the phone with her than

I had the night before, reassuring her that everything was still fine and telling her I loved her. And after that I spent an hour or so catching up with my notes, trying to see what I'd forgotten to do but nothing sprang out at me. Then I decided to simply have dinner in and I called up my nice, friendly waiter guy and ordered a decent steak and chips which I devoured with alacrity – it was very good as American steaks usually are! – and then watched a little mindless American TV before collapsing into bed and sleeping the sleep of the just, lulled by the gentle rocking of the huge ship.

CHAPTER 17

MOST OF WEDNESDAY

I got up early the next morning, remembering that I'd gone to bed at 7.30, very early indeed for me, but reckoning I must have needed the sleep as I felt reinvigorated. I was pleased that I hadn't needed to resort to the whisky I'd brought to help me sleep. I rang down for breakfast and did my usual morning stuff. My breakfast arrived soon after and I gobbled it all up, feeling even better afterwards. I looked at my watch and saw it was now 7.00, so it'd be 10 in England, a good time to ring Alan, which I did. He answered almost immediately and I asked him at once if he'd managed to get into Alexei's flat yet.

'It should be happening as we speak,' he said.

'Good. So you managed to get that warrant?'

'Indeed, we did, with Sir M's help. And I took you up on your suggestion of using Sam Bullock to get in. I presume your asking is because you know we picked him up yesterday?'

'Yes, Sir M told me last night. How is he doing now, by the way?'

'You mean, after a night without sleep? Better than I expected, to be honest. I reckon he'll be a tough nut to crack.'

'Everyone has their own breaking point. Keep softening him up for me though. And, if you get anything particularly interesting from his flat, I hope you'll let me know. I look forward to hearing about your adventures in detail when I get back.'

'I'm sure they're not as exciting as yours, Jack.'

'Nothing exciting's happened yet. It's just been planning so far. By the way, did Sir M tell you I'm hoping to be back within about 48 hours?'

'Yes, boss.'

'OK, bye then and don't forget to keep me informed of what you find in Alexei's flat.'

'Bye, Jack. No, I won't forget and good luck at your end and do try not to blow up too many ships,' which made me chuckle as I hung up.

Now I needed to get up to the bridge pronto to find out two important things and to do that I needed Tom. So I rang him and he answered quickly, saying, 'Be right there, sir.' And he was although he looked a little more dishevelled than usual. Probably I'd woken him up. I told him where I needed to go and apologised if I'd woken him but he just said, 'Yes, sir. Follow me.'

So I did and not long afterwards we arrived and things seemed to be even more hectic there than the day before but I spotted the Admiral at once and went straight up to him to where he was talking to someone sitting at a computer. He turned at my approach and said, 'Hope you slept well, Jack. You're up early.'

'Yes, I did, sir, thank you. I think you can probably guess why I'm here. I'd like to find out first if we arrived at our destination last night on time or if the storm delayed us. And second, what the status of the buoy is.'

'To answer your first question: yes, we did and no, the storm didn't delay us. It would take a really major hurricane to do that and this is just a typical Atlantic storm. As for your second about the buoy: Bradley had a small technical problem to resolve with it and we didn't manage to fly it off the ship until 6 am this morning. But it's now working fine and should be clearly audible to the Virago.'

'That's very good news, sir. I don't think that should affect my basic timing at all. And is the Virago doing anything about it?'

'No, nothing at all. It's still just sitting there.'

'Yes, that's what I expected to happen. But, if it does move to investigate it, I'd like to be informed at once as it means I'll have to change my game plan.'

'Of course, Jack. You'll be the first to know.'

'And now, thinking ahead a bit, I'm sorry but I'm going to have to love you and leave you pretty soon after I get back, probably very early tomorrow morning, and I was wondering if I could borrow one of your fighters again then? I need to get back to England in a hurry to interview the mastermind behind all this.'

'You've got him then, I presume? You didn't tell us about that.'

'Yes, indeed, sir, but only since yesterday,' I said, 'and I didn't think it was relevant to your mission.'

'No,' he said, 'I suppose not. And yes, of course you can. We'll have it ready. I understand you've already talked to Chuck and my ABM team.'

'Yes, indeed, sir. And, hopefully, things are about as well prepared as they can be. And thanks very much again, sir.'

'My pleasure, Jack. Although we're not only doing all this for you, you know. I have my orders and it's in the best interests of my country too.'

'I know, sir, but you really have looked after me very well.'

'It's the least we could do.' And that was the end of that short but very satisfactory conversation. I went back to my cabin now, shown the way by Tom and wondering what I could do for the next 12 hours or so until 9 pm. Then I decided I needed to make a couple more phone calls, first to Sir M to bring him up to date which I did in short order and second to Sam Bullock to thank him for his help in getting into Alexei's flat. But he waved off my thanks, saying, 'I understand you're sailing the high seas out of my jurisdiction, thank God,' which made me smile and I hung up on another high.

Then I decided to update my notes which took me about another hour after which I rang Tom again and asked him what I'd missed on the tour yesterday and he said 'Not much, actually. Visitors are often interested in the workings of the laundry room and the ratings' quarters. Oh, and the engine room, of course.'

'Would I get to see the reactor?'

'No, I'm afraid not. That's heavily shielded for very good reasons, as I'm sure you can imagine. There's basically just a bunch of teccies looking at computer screens.'

'Oh, OK. Doesn't sound terribly exciting. I think I'll give the rest of the tour a miss then. But I would like to go back to my cutter at some point later on.'

'Sure, sir. After lunch, maybe?'

'Sounds good to me. Shall we say 2 pm, which reminds me, have we changed time zones yet?'

'No, sir, not yet. So we'll say 2 o'clock, shall we?' I agreed and hung up.

So I had another few hours to fill but then Alan called, sounding excited. 'Guess what, boss?' he started.

'You should know by now I hate guessing games. Just tell me.'

'We have just started processing Alexei's flat and it's a real treasure trove. So is his mobile which has lots of encrypted calls back to mother Russia, to the Kremlin no less.'

'Can you decipher them?'

'No, not yet but I thought you'd want to know.'

'So what treasure have you found in his flat then?'

'Well, Gloria has managed to crack his laptop, not that difficult really she says. He was probably relying on the heavy security around his flat, multiple alarm systems, pressure pads and God knows what all.'

'Yes, go on,' I said impatiently now.

'It's got all the information she needed to access his

other accounts with all his hidden millions. He was using different names again for them which was why she had such difficulty finding them. At least this means that you can threaten him with embargoing his source of funds, freezing his assets in other words, which I would imagine will piss off his masters back home.'

'Yes, that's true. Anything else?'

'Yes, I said that his flat was a treasure trove. It's actually more like an Aladdin's cave of everything a modern spy might need, from highly miniaturised cameras to advanced radio equipment. It's going to take us ages to process everything.'

'Anything relating to my present mission?' I asked.

'Well, we can now prove beyond doubt that he went up to Liverpool on the 12th February. It's in his diary which we found too.'

'Good. That should all be enough to break him hopefully. Remember I need anything relating to the Virago. Keep up the good work. Speak to you later.' And I disconnected.

A little bit later, while I was updating my notes, Toby also rang, sounding excited too. 'Guess who's Alexei's uncle?' he said.

'Oh, no, not you too! Just tell me, Toby.'

'Only Medvedev!' he said, sounding a bit nonplussed by my response.

'The Prime Minister,' a bit disappointed. 'So it could be his operation,' I said.

'We think not. He never does anything without consulting his boss first.'

I cheered up when I heard this. But then I thought of something else. 'Could he be the source of the funds?'

'Again we think not. He doesn't have easy access to the millions an operation like this would cost. We reckon it must come from the very top.'

'OK. Thanks a lot, Toby. More grist to the mill.' I went on to detail what Alan had told me they'd found in his flat and Toby was suitably impressed. And that was pretty much the end of that conversation. I wondered who else would call but, in the event, nobody did and I just twiddled my thumbs for a bit.

Then I decided to lie down and I must have fallen asleep again because, when I woke up, it was 12.30 and I realised I was hungry so I called down to the kitchen and asked whether they could do me a decent curry. The guy there sounded a bit miffed that I even had to ask. We discussed what type of meat I wanted in it (beef) and how hot I wanted it (medium) and he said it'd be with me in a few minutes. I had time to wash my face and hands and tidy my desk before he knocked. I ate as usual with relish and wondering how much weight I must be putting on and leaving my tray outside the room to be collected, I sat down waiting for Tom.

He took me back to the hangar with the cutter in it and I told him that I hoped that was the end of his duties towards me and thanked him effusively for all his help. But he shrugged off my thanks, saying, 'It really was my pleasure, sir. I wish all my customers were like you,' and then disappeared to do whatever his normal duties were. I walked over to the cutter and saw a few of Chuck's men still working on it. They greeted me with a cheerful, 'Hi, there, Mr Sanderson.'

'Have you nearly finished, guys?' I asked.

'Yes, thanks. Just putting the finishing touches to everything,' one of them said.

'Where's Chuck?'

'Probably bonking one of his girl friends,' another said and I chuckled, recognising the unlikelihood of such a scenario but also again the closeness of them as a team.

'How do you propose to get this thing in the water and then get us into it?'

'Oh, we'll all probably be rappelling down the sides of the carrier to keep it steady,' a third said, but then, his face split into a huge grin and I realised, much to my relief, that he was joking. I really didn't fancy the idea of rappelling at my age. Those days were long gone for me. 'No, don't worry, sir,' he continued, recognising my dismay, 'it'll be much simpler than that. Those doors there,' and he pointed, 'open almost straight into the ocean. We'll all be aboard and given a gentle shove and we'll be there.'

'Thank God for that,' I said. 'You had me worried there for a second. Do you know if our target has moved at all?'

'No, our latest information is that it's still sitting there.'

'Good. And one final question: Is my interpreter around?'

'Gerry, you're needed,' one of them called out and the

dark-skinned guy I'd noticed before popped his head out of the innards of the boat.

'Who needs me?' he called out.

'I do,' I called back.

'Oh, yes, Mr Sanderson. Can you give me a minute, sir, to finish up what I was doing?' and he disappeared back inside so I sat down on an empty oil drum and waited for him. He wasn't long and, when he reappeared, he asked, 'Now, what can I do for you, sir?'

'I think I'll almost certainly need you,' I said, 'and I'd like to run over the way I see the conversation going with these maniacs.'

'Yes, sir. Shall we go somewhere a little quieter?'

'Sure, can I see around the cutter, do you think? Is there anywhere suitable on board?'

'Yes, sure to both questions.' After hauling me up on a rope attached to its stern, easily done, I might add, as he was very strong, he took me on a quick tour of the boat. It was bigger than I expected inside with ten bunk beds neatly made up in the biggest cabin, all of them covered with weaponry and personal comms equipment, some of which I recognised and some of which I didn't. Then he showed me two much smaller cabins and said, 'This is where you'll be sleeping, sir,' about one of them. 'Chuck will be in the other.' After that he showed me up to the bridge and closed the door behind him. Suddenly it was quiet. I looked around with curiosity but, apart from the large steering wheel and a number of computer screens, all blank now, there wasn't much more I could have put a name to.

'This do?' he asked now.

'Perfect,' I said. 'As I said, I wanted to run over a potential scenario for the way the conversation might go.' And I proceeded to do exactly that. He didn't turn a hair at my suggestions but said, 'That shouldn't be a problem at all, sir. It's all pretty straightforward in Arabic.'

'And it won't matter what type of Arabic they speak?'

'No, not at all, sir. I speak all the major dialects.'

'That's what I wanted to hear. Thanks a lot, Gerry.'

'My pleasure, sir. We like to keep our customers satisfied,' which made me grin. I really liked these guys' sense of humour.

'Now, Gerry, do you think you could track down Chuck for me?'

'Sure thing, sir.' And he pulled a mobile out of his pocket and dialled a number. 'Here he is.'

'Chuck, hi!' I said. 'I'm at the cutter now and have spoken to a number of your guys who have reassured me about a few things. I was wondering if you were free?'

'I'm just finishing off calibrating the comms signals with the ABM guys but I won't be long. I was going to come down there as soon as I've finished up here anyway. Can you wait for me there?'

'Yes, sure. Your guys are keeping me amused.'

'Good. See you soon then.' And he disconnected.

I decided to stay on board to do a bit more exploring and went first back to the cabin that had been pointed out as mine. It actually had a functioning toilet, sink and shower in it and I did my business and then left. After all, I wouldn't be in it very long, would I? Then I just wandered around, peering into every dark corner, and quickly found the boxes where the munitions were to be stored while we were at sea and admired their workmanship. I didn't bother going down into the hold because it was very dark down there and I didn't have a torch with me. When I thought I knew the interior of the boat as well as possible, I just went back up to the bridge and sat in a comfy chair waiting for Chuck. God knew where Gerry had gone.

But Chuck dutifully appeared not long after and I asked him first about communicating with the fighters.

'All sorted,' he said but I wanted a bit more detail than that.

'Will I be able to talk to them myself, if needed?'

'Yes, sure. No problem. They're on a dedicated frequency. I'll show you how it works when we're at sea.'

'That's a relief,' I said. 'And what about the ABM lot?'

'They're on a different one. Don't worry, Jack. I'm pretty sure we have everything under control.'

'That's good, Chuck. I'm glad to hear it. I'm sorry if I seem a bit of a worrywart but I'm always like this before a big operation.'

'Oh, I don't blame you. Check everything and then check again is our motto. I have just one question for you: do you tend to get seasick?'

Now this was something I hadn't considered. What would happen to the operation if I was laid up in bed with an acute attack of vomiting? But I answered as truthfully as I could, 'I haven't actually ever been at sea during a big storm to the best of my recollection but no, I'm not normally seasick.'

'Perhaps you should take some Dramamine then, just to be on the safe side.'

'Yes, OK, but not too much. I don't want to get drowsy.'

'We always carry plenty with us. You'll be fine, I'm sure. It's nothing to be ashamed of.'

'Thanks again, Chuck.'

'My pleasure.'

'Are we still all go for 9pm?'

'It depends on the Admiral. But I haven't heard any different. We'll certainly be ready for then.'

'That's good enough for me. OK, Chuck. Well, I think that's everything sorted from my perspective too. If I go back to my cabin now, can you send somebody to come and get me at, say, 8.00, sorry 20 hundred hours? I'll have my bag with me which is quite heavy. Oh yes, that's something I haven't told you. I'll be leaving you guys pretty much immediately on my return to go back to England. I have an emergency to deal with there connected with our operation.'

'To answer your question: yes sure, but maybe you should aim to be here a little earlier. Say we collect you at 7.30 in case we're given the go-ahead to leave a bit earlier.'

'Sure. Less time to spend on biting my fingernails, eh?'

He chuckled and replied, 'Yes, I guess so.'

I walked slowly back to my cabin, only once getting lost this time, thinking of all the things that could still go wrong and hoping I hadn't forgotten anything important but reassured by the obvious professionalism of the team I'd be taking with me. When I got there, I packed slowly and methodically and then looked at my watch. Still only 4.25. Another 3 hours to kill. Fortunately I remembered to ring Pamela, told her everything was fine and then had to listen to a long and involved story about how one of her friends was getting divorced after 20 years of marriage, which I did patiently, making all the appropriate noises, I hoped. Then I decided to eat early and ordered a light meal of an omelette with vegetables on the side and, after I'd eaten, decided to lie down for a bit and actually managed to doze for a while even though the adrenalin was starting to kick in.

CHAPTER 18

WEDNESDAY 7.30 PM TO 10.00 AM THURSDAY

A discreet tap on the door at 7.30 on the dot was enough to wake me and I went to it to find one of Chuck's team outside (I still hadn't come to terms with all their names). 'Give me a moment,' I said and went into the bathroom and washed my face in cold water which revivified me. Then I came out and handed him my bag, checking the room carefully to make sure I hadn't forgotten anything as I probably wouldn't be coming back. After that it was straight off to the cutter where I was hauled up again and which I found to be in a state of controlled chaos with Chuck's team all there in the big cabin, trying on their body armour and checking weapons. I thanked the guy for carrying my bag and then carried it to my own cabin, unpacking just a few essentials and putting it away in the small wardrobe. Then I went to find Chuck and, not surprisingly, found him on the bridge, doing something arcane on one of the computers.

'Hi, there!' he called out cheerily and I wondered if anything ever rattled him but replied with the same words to his greeting. 'Ready for the off?' he said now.

'As ready as I'll ever be,' I said.

'I'm just plotting our course,' he said.

'Will it be you actually driving the boat?'

'Not all the time, no. We're all qualified to do it. We'll be taking it in shifts.' He finished what he was doing and then turned to face me. 'Would you like one of those Dramamine now? They're rather a special variant of them which shouldn't make you drowsy. I'm expecting a fairly large swell outside.'

'Yes, OK,' I said and he handed me a packet of large, blue pills.

'They're not Viagra, I hope,' I said, trying to be funny, and at least he had the grace to laugh.

'No, they're not, actually,' he said so I dry swallowed one of them.

Then I asked if he could show me the comms gear which we'd be using to communicate between ourselves and the fighters and the ABM guys. Like a magician pulling a rabbit out of a hat, he put his hand in his pocket and brought out a tiny device, about the size of a hearing aid, on a cord which had an equally small microphone on it, the size of a small lozenge. None of the old-fashioned, bulky gear for these guys. I was impressed and told Chuck so.

'And how do we change frequencies?' I asked now.

He showed me a small switch, fixed to the microphone, and said, 'Just turn it to the left if you need to speak to the fighters and right for the ABM guys. The central position is for us to communicate with each other. That's what it's on now.'

'Can I try it out?'

'Sure, but, remember, the fighter jocks won't be in the air yet.'

So I turned the switch to the right and said in a normal voice, 'This is Jack Sanderson calling the ABM team.'

A voice answered immediately, saying, 'This is the ABM team. Hello, Mr Sanderson. What can we do for you?' it came through as clear as a bell on the tiny earpiece.

'Just testing the comms gear for my mission. Seems to be working fine,' I said.

'A wise precaution, sir. If you're happy, I'll leave you now.'

'OK. Over and out.'

'We won't be able to test the connection between us and the fighters until we're about 4 hours out but I checked it earlier and it was fine.'

'That's good enough for me. Like I said, it's an impressive piece of kit.'

'Yes, we like it. You can keep that one. I have another for myself.'

'Thanks a lot, Chuck,' I said pocketing it. 'I hope that's the last piece of the jigsaw.'

'Don't forget, Jack. Situations like this quite often spin out of control and we all have to improvise.'

'That's exactly what my boss keeps telling me. I know it very well. But I feel much better now I've got you watching my back.' And that was the end of that particular conversation. Now it was just a question of sitting around waiting for the go signal which finally came at about 8.45 with a call from the Admiral himself.

'Everything's set up at our end. You're free to leave now,' he said, adding, 'Good luck. We'll be watching your progress anxiously.'

'Thank you very much, sir, for everything. Get your men keeping an eye on the satellite images, won't you? If they see anything at all anomalous, they must let us know at once.'

'Of course, Jack. See you later then.'

'Don't forget I'll have to leave pretty promptly after I get back.'

'Don't worry. I haven't forgotten. Bye for now.'

Chuck had been listening in and now radioed his men to say they were leaving now and there was a flurry of activity inside the boat with most of his team scampering around it, which had clearly been well rehearsed. The boat was wheeled down to the big exit doors which opened slowly, showing a ramp leading down to the sea outside. But, before I knew it, they were all back on board and we were being shoved outside. Somehow we slid down the ramp and then we were in the water, being tossed this way and that by seemingly enormous waves. However, Chuck quickly started the engines and guided us away from our huge parent ship into the open ocean.

Quite soon we were on our way properly, with the little boat skipping over the waves effortlessly, and Chuck turned to me and said, 'Why don't you go back to your cabin now and try to rest a bit? There won't be anything to see for several hours now.'

'OK. I'll try although I don't think I'll be able to rest much.'

'But still it's worth a try, isn't it?' he said now.

So I meekly did as he suggested, passing through the big cabin where most of the team were already snoring away lustily like every professional soldier in history before a battle, and, in spite of rather a lot of rolling around in the swell (or was it because of it?), managed to doze a bit. The Dramamine, or whatever it was, had appeared to do a very good job because, when I was bleeped by Chuck, I didn't feel drowsy or sick at all. He said that we had gone through the 4-hour mark and were now in contact with the fighters and invited me to come up to the bridge to talk to them myself so that they could hear my voice.

I did that and found the reception as clear as a bell. They said they were patrolling the sky far above the Virago and would stay on the same courses until they were no longer needed. I asked them how long it would take them to get down to sea level and they said, 'A couple of minutes max'. I thanked them and then said 'Roger and out'. They acknowledged and we all clicked off.

'Phew!' I said to Chuck now. 'Hopefully, that really is the last piece of the jigsaw. Thanks for inviting me up here to talk to them.'

'Would you like to stay now you're up and about?' he asked. 'You can admire my seamanship.'

This made me laugh but I said, 'Yes, I'd love to stay.'

So I did and the last two hours of the journey went very quickly with Chuck giving me a comprehensive course in basic seamanship, most of which went straight in one ear and out of the other. I knew he was trying to distract me from worrying about the operation but I was grateful to him for trying.

And then suddenly I saw something on the horizon. 'Is that it?' I asked but I could see from the huge derricks on board that it must be. 'Yes. Battle stations, men!' Chuck called out now and there was a flurry of activity as everyone went to their assigned spot, except for Gerry who came up to the bridge to be with me. But he too was now dressed in full combat gear with his face blackened and carrying a fearsome array of weaponry. I looked at my watch and saw it was now 2.45 – a perfect time to catch them at their sleepiest although I knew that we would have been on their radar for some time. I checked that I had my pistol nestling in my belt next to my back bone and felt its reassuring but well-hidden bulk.

We were now coming up rapidly to them and Chuck told Gerry to get them on the radio. He tried to do this but there was no reply. 'This is USS Coast Guard Vessel Oklahoma calling the Virago. Please reply,' he repeated but again there was no response. I wasn't that surprised but we'd practised this scenario already and Gerry said into the microphone, 'We're coming alongside you now. We need to talk to you. There is no reason to be alarmed,' repeating the message in Arabic.

This provoked a reaction finally and I heard through

the speakers a rumbly voice say, 'Go away,' in a pronounced Arabic accent.

Now I took the microphone from Gerry and said, 'Would it help if we used my interpreter to talk? We just want to invite the master of your vessel on board so we can talk.'

'Go away,' the voice said again.

'We're not going anywhere, not until we can have a proper talk man-to-man,' I said.

And that was where everything started to go pear-shaped. We were almost alongside now and my conciliatory words only elicited a volley of rapid gunfire from the Virago, the bullets just bouncing off the hardened glass of our big window, thank God. They had obviously carried no weight at all with them. Chuck said calmly into his throat mike, 'Return fire, lads,' and suddenly the much bigger ship was enveloped in a huge hail of bullets. I saw a couple of their men fall into the ocean, hit by our snipers who all seemed to be concealed behind barriers of different sorts. I wondered why our heavy machine gun on the foredeck wasn't being used and then realised we were too close to the much bigger ship and any gunfire from it would have simply passed over the top of it as there was no angle to shoot from. My adrenalin was now in overdrive and I was trying to predict which way the battle would go.

'Now will you please take our invitation seriously?' I said into the ship-to-ship mike in a lull in the gunfire and then asked Gerry to translate my words which he did calmly.

'We are not afraid to die,' the same voice said now in Arabic, which was rapidly translated by Gerry. I recognised this tone of voice, that of the true fanatic, and knew at that moment that things could only end in extreme violence.

But then I heard through the open door of the bridge the sound which I'd prayed I wouldn't, the low rumble of heavy steel doors opening and I knew that they were preparing to fire one of their missiles. Chuck must have heard it too as he immediately called the two men back who'd somehow dropped into the ocean unseen and were preparing to mine the cable-laying ship. I knew this was a good move on his part as we'd have to leave very soon now if the fighters were going to do their jobs properly.

I called them up and said, 'We need you to destroy the ship urgently now. They're about to fire a missile.'

'Yes, sir,' came the brief, laconic reply.

Then I called up the ABM team and said as calmly as I could, 'Prepare to launch, please.'

'Already done, sir,' came the swift reply. 'We're watching the action via the satellite.'

'Thank you,' I said and disconnected.

Next I saw us moving slightly so we were angled away from the Virago and we waited a minute or so before I saw the two men in black frogmen's suits climbing swiftly up the ropes dangling from the back of the cutter. I turned away then since I wanted to watch what was happening on the enemy ship and as soon as they were, apparently safely, on board, Chuck opened the engines up to full power and zoomed away from the Virago. We had gone only about one hundred yards, however, before the fighters zoomed into sight and released their own missiles. But just before they did, I saw the much bigger missile launch from the Virago on a pillar of fire into the dark sky. Now I could only pray. Then the fighters' smaller missiles hit the ship and everything turned into a vision of hell, a total inferno. They struck the vessel squarely amidships and suddenly it became totally engulfed in flames until the fire must have reached the other nuclear missile and set off a truly massive explosion and that was when it rapidly broke up. It was the end of the ship and it sank very quickly. I knew there could be no survivors and wasn't surprised when Chuck continued to zoom away from the maelstrom.

We ourselves hadn't got off unscathed though as I heard Chuck say now, 'Damage report, please,' and his men reported back with a number of problems. But I couldn't concern myself with those now as I was too busy scanning the sky to see if I could spot the missile. The next thing I knew was when Chuck yelled into his mike, 'Hang on, lads!', and then we were hit by a massive wave. It appeared to be at least 10 metres high, far higher than anything on our little cutter, and we almost turned over. In spite of the fact that I was hanging onto something, I was knocked right off my feet and hit my head on something cold and hard. We were only saved, I believe, by the brilliant seamanship of Chuck who must have realised it was coming after the massive explosion on the Virago and turned into it. But then we were through it and into a patch of relatively calm water. I felt the back of my head and could feel a lump coming but didn't think I had concussion as I wasn't seeing double or anything like that. But then I'd always had a hard skull. I heard Chuck say, 'Are you OK, Jack?' but didn't bother responding, pulling myself to my feet and continuing to scan the sky for anything untoward. And suddenly I saw a brilliant flash of light, so high that it came from way above the cloud cover and so bright that it actually hurt my retinas and I had to look away. I realised at once what had happened. One of the ABM missiles must have hit its target and ignited the nuclear explosive it was carrying — either that or its fuel tanks. So it had worked! We were now in the clear, thank God.

I now focussed on where the ship had sunk and saw the two fighters circling low above where it had been, obviously taking photos of the scene to show their superiors later. I radioed them and congratulated them on a job well done but they just replied, 'All in a day's work, sir.'

Then I radioed the ABM team and said, 'Good shooting, men,' and they said, 'We got lucky, Jack. That was all.' But I knew it wasn't just luck on their part. Now I looked at my watch and saw it was only 3.14. Less than half an hour to create all that mayhem! Amazing! Now I turned to Chuck and asked, 'How are we doing?'

'Reasonably well, considering,' he replied, concentrating on getting us as far away as possible from the scene of the sinking. But then he called up Gerry and asked him to take over. When he arrived, he said to me, 'Now we can talk. How are you going to explain this mess to your masters back home?' he asked.

'I'll just have to tell them the truth, I guess. I reckon the terrorists would never have negotiated and would have received instructions to release their wretched missiles at once if they were ever challenged. I expect they'll say it was a tragic accident at sea and leave it at that. But all's well that ends well, no?'

'Not quite. I lost a man, unfortunately. His name was Ryan and he had a family back in Wisconsin. He was one of the frogmen who were deputed to mine the ship and he was hit by a stray bullet in the last flurry of firing from the Virago. He wasn't wearing body armour, of course, just his wetsuit.'

'Oh, no! I'm so sorry, Chuck,' I said now. 'I had no idea.' I knew how close a team they were and how keenly they would feel the loss of a member.

'The fortunes of war,' he replied and I didn't know what else I could say so I just stayed silent. Suddenly the day seemed to have become much darker and more meaningless. But Chuck's natural insouciance quickly reasserted itself and he said, 'But yes, that's probably the way I'd play it too. Why don't you go back to your cabin and rest a bit now, Jack? I don't expect there'll be any more excitement for about another three hours when we rendezvous with the carrier. And before you ask, they're steaming towards us at full speed as we speak.'

Another thing I wasn't aware of, I thought sourly. But I could see the sense in it. Now there was, of course, no reason why the carrier couldn't come much closer, especially with a dead man on board and unspecified problems with the cutter. So I said, 'Yes, I think I might do that. Thanks for keeping an old man's weaknesses in mind, Chuck. I'll get out of your way now,' which at least made him grin wryly. So I left and on going through the main cabin, I found a much more sombre mood than I'd done before. I commiserated with the team and they took my sorrow at face value with no recriminations, to my relief. When I was back in my little cabin, I felt the lump on my head again and it was still very sore but I didn't think it would prejudice my return to England. So I just lay down with my fairly dismal thoughts and philosophised about the pointlessness of war, not able to sleep at all. 'What could I have done differently?' was the question going round and round like a hamster in my mind. But no answer came to me and I finally decided to put the question aside for another day. Only then was I able to rest a bit.

And, before I knew it, I heard a knock on my door and, when I opened it, one of the team was outside with a message from Chuck. 'About 15 minutes till we arrive, sir,' he said. I thanked him and washed my face and hands, not forgetting to go to the toilet, and repacked my luggage. Then I just sat there and waited. And very soon I heard us being winched up the ramp and came out to watch from the bridge. An amazing sight greeted me. There appeared to be a full guard of honour in the hangar with the Admiral at its head.

I was first off the cutter at Chuck's insistence and, as I was helped down from our boat onto the hangar floor, everyone waiting for us broke into spontaneous applause. I had no idea how to behave. Were they all really applauding me after the mess I'd made of everything? But I was saved by the Admiral who came straight up to me and shook my hand warmly. 'Well done, Jack!' he said, 'Your plan actually worked! Thanks very much indeed for saving us from complete meltdown back home.' I was extremely nonplussed by this and just muttered something about it being very much a team effort, which it certainly was. I couldn't have done it without all the support from the carrier, I pointed out, but the Admiral just pooh-poohed me, saying, 'Yes, but you were the one to first identify the very real threat, weren't you?' And now I was really stumped. What on earth could I say to that? But I was saved form saying anything again by the Admiral who said, 'Come, Jack. Our President is waiting to thank you in person.'

Now I was totally gobsmacked but I followed him meekly back into a small lift which took us almost directly up to his quarters where I noticed his private phone dangling off the receiver. I picked it up at his insistence and said, 'Hello? Mr President?', berating myself at once for the idiocy of my words. But then I heard the familiar voice say, 'Hello. Is this Mr Jack Sanderson?' and, when I'd agreed that that was me, it said, 'I believe that my country owes you a profound debt of gratitude, not only for identifying the threat in the first place but also in the execution of a very dangerous and difficult mission, which, fortunately, ended in total success. And I'd like you to come to the White House, not for the first time, I believe,' *(referring to the incident I recounted in my former memoir The Dirty Bomb Affair)* 'so that I can thank you in person after you've sorted out your little problem in England.' His words immediately made me realise how closely he must be in touch with my PM if he knew about Alexei.

'Yes, well, thank you very much indeed for your kind invitation,' I said in reply, 'but you must realise, sir, how much of a team effort it was. I honestly didn't actually do much on the mission itself at all except for get in the way of the SEALS who were with me. And I had to rely on the fighter pilots to sink the Virago and the ABM team on the carrier to down the terrorists' wretched missile.'

'Yes, yes,' came the impatient reply, 'and they will all be rewarded in the fullness of time. However, my offer still stands as, without you, we would probably have had no electricity grid to speak of. So goodbye, Jack, and I look forward to welcoming you to Washington in due course.' And, after I'd said bye, that was the end of that conversation.

The Admiral had been listening to my half of the conversation and said now, 'What's really bugging you, Jack?'

'The fact that we lost a good man,' I said miserably. 'I think it's the first time on a mission that's happened to me.'

'It's what they signed up for, Jack. They all know the risks and that they're not immortal. And what better way to die for a professional soldier than to go out in a blaze of glory. He will get a good send off and his widow will be well provided for, you can be sure of that.'

'Since you put it like that.....,' I said uncertainly. 'OK, Admiral, you have reassured me somewhat.' I finished honestly.

'Good. Now rejoice in the overall success of your mission.'

'Yes, sir,' I said now, more positively. 'Now, sir, there is a very little something I'd like to give you as a small token of my appreciation for everything you have done for me but I'm afraid I left it in my bag.'

'Oh, goodie. A present. I love presents,' he said now just like a small child, clapping his hands together, which made me laugh outright. I hadn't realised he had a sense of humour. Then he grinned at me and said, 'That's more like it, Jack.' I thought again what a good commander he must be to work for. 'Actually, I was going to come with you anyway to wave you off unless I can persuade you to stay a bit longer on my boat.'

'No, thanks. I really must be getting back.' And so we left his cabin and went back to the flight deck where I met my new pilot, another young chap called Sam. He came down from his fighter and shook my hand warmly, saying in a warm, languid Texan drawl, 'It'll be a great pleasure to fly you back to England, sir.' I took to him at once.

'Is my bag here?' I asked him.

'Yes, sir, all safely stowed away on the plane.'

'I'm so sorry. Would you mind getting somebody to

take it out? There's something in it I want to give the Admiral.'

'I can do that myself,' he said and disappeared for a few seconds, reappearing with my bag. I opened it and took out the bottle of whisky, still unopened, and presented it to the Admiral with a flourish, saying, 'This is the real thing, sir. I don't think you can get it in the States. I bought it on a recent trip to Scotland.'

He examined the label with interest and said, 'No, I don't think you can. I'm very partial to the occasional drop of single malt. Thank you very much indeed, Jack. Consider all debts squared away.'

'I'm sure a whole bunch of jet fuel plus a few missiles are worth more than a bottle of whisky, sir,' I said and he grinned at me.

Then he shook my hand and said, 'I'll leave you now in Sam's capable hands. Have a good flight.' And he walked off, clutching my bottle. And that was the last I saw of him.

I was pleased that I'd thought of giving him the bottle and now there was just one other thing to do before I left, to ring Sir M. So, as soon as I was in the small quiet room getting suited up, I did that, bringing him quickly up to date with just the salient facts and getting him to promise to tell Alan. He listened without comment, fortunately, but I knew he'd be on the blower to the PM after I hung up. Before I signed off, I looked at my watch and saw it was now about 7.30, so it should be about 10.30 British time if my maths was correct. Then I asked him if he could ring Lakenheath and tell them roughly what time I'd be arriving and ask them if I could have a driver waiting to take me home in my car as I knew I'd be too tired to drive myself. I could feel all the adrenalin draining away now and he just said, 'Sure Jack. What time do you think you'll be able to come in?' and I told him very approximately and he just said, 'OK. See you soon,' and we left it there. I thought I'd wait to ring Pamela until I got back to England. Then it was just a question of finishing the suiting up and getting everything checked and remarkably quickly, we were in the air. Sam seemed to have waived the necessity of going through all the rules and strictures knowing that I'd been through all that recently.

CHAPTER 19

THE REST OF THURSDAY

The flight passed quickly with Sam's expert piloting keeping everything smooth and I managed to doze a bit. I even ate a sandwich, provided by a kind Sam, after we went subsonic again and didn't need the oxygen, which took the edge off my hunger. But then only about 2 1/2 hours later we landed at Lakenheath with Sam explaining that we'd had a decent tailwind behind us. And after I'd said goodbye to him and got myself unsuited, I found my car waiting for me outside the hangar into which we'd been towed, with a chirpy American driver saying, 'Where to, sir?'

I gave the chap my address in Highgate and said, 'it's in the Satnav under 'home',' and he found it very quickly. I looked behind me and noticed a US Air Force jeep, following us off the base and said, 'Why have we got an escort?'

'It's not exactly an escort, sir. It's to take me home after I've dropped you off.'

'Silly me. It's been a very long night.' Now I felt I could ring Pamela and, when she picked up her mobile, said, 'Hello, darling, it's time to kick all those randy young studs out of the flat. I'm back in England.'

She squealed with delight as I'd hoped and then laughed and said, 'I wish! When will you be arriving?'

'In a couple of hours, traffic permitting. I warn you though: I'm very hungry and, after I've eaten, will need to crash out. I didn't get much rest last night.'

'We'll see about that,' she replied, giggling. 'Lunch will be on the table.' And we disconnected. I dozed for the rest of the journey but woke up properly when we got to London and had quite an interesting chat with my driver who, it turned out, had rather a fascinating CV, having done a wide range of other jobs before deciding to join the Air Force. But then we arrived home and I got out lugging my slightly less heavy suitcase. I thanked my driver who, at once, jumped out of my car, transferred to the jeep and sped off. I decided to leave my car in one of the parking bays outside the flat, ready to take me back to the office, rather than parking it in the garage. Then it was just a question of going up in the lift and knocking on my door.

Pamela opened it immediately, saying, 'The conquering hero returns! Was that an American Air Force jeep I saw arriving behind you?'

'No questions, please! Not now. I'm knackered. Can we eat now?' I said.

'Yes, of course, poor darling.' And I followed her through into the dining area where we had a delicious lunch. I could see her bursting with questions but also knew that I wouldn't be able to answer any of them as the mission was still absolutely top secret. So, as soon as we finished, I excused myself and went into our bedroom where I just collapsed onto the bed and slept (in my clothes) for the next 9 hours. I'd forgotten how badly jet lag can hit you, especially travelling east to west. But I knew it wasn't only jet lag that had exhausted me.

When I finally got up, I had a quick shower and, feeling much better in clean clothes, went out to find Pamela. She was in the sitting room watching TV and laughing at one of our favourite sitcoms. I looked at my watch but then remembered I hadn't changed it since the carrier before everything had happened. 'What time is it?' I asked, forgetting that there was a clock on the mantelpiece. Perhaps the bump on my head was more serious than I'd thought.

'Only coming up to 10 o'clock,' she said. 'Have you been travelling?' she asked now perspicaciously.

'Yes, actually,' I said. 'But please no more questions. It really is very top secret.'

'It always is,' she said, rather bitterly now. 'But if I suggested you had just returned from America, would I be very wide of the mark? You can just answer yes or no.'

Then I remembered what she was talking about. That blasted American jeep she had seen! She must have been waiting for me, watching through the big picture window in the living room which overlooked the front of the flats. I decided she deserved something in return for being a grass widow for the past few days and said, 'You clever little minx! Yes, you're quite right is the answer to your question,' I said, bending the truth only slightly. 'But no tattling to any of your friends about my little trip, OK? Now talk to me and tell me what you've been up to since I left.'

'OK, boss,' she said now with a self-satisfied grin. 'How about eating while we talk? I haven't had supper yet. I've been waiting for you to wake up.'

I realised now that I was indeed very hungry again and said, 'An excellent idea, darling! I could eat a horse.'

'No horse meat on the menu tonight, I'm afraid. Maybe tomorrow.' That was one of the reasons I loved her so much. We had very similar senses of humour. And she buzzed off into the kitchen and soon reappeared with one of my favourite English meals (toad-in-the-hole with decent gravy) cooked to perfection along with an expensive bottler of Malbec. We polished off everything in short order, with her chattering away between mouthfuls about what she'd been doing.

When we'd finished, I offered to do the washing up (my job in the house anyway) and let her go back to her TV watching. After that, I joined her on the sofa for a bit and then rather shyly suggested we went to bed. 'I thought you'd never ask,' she said and disappeared off to the bathroom to get herself ready for bed.

We had some marvellous hanky-panky and, just before she turned over and went to sleep, I said totally honestly, 'That was exactly what the doctor ordered. I really don't deserve you, do I?'

'You're telling me, mate!' she replied in her authentic Cockney accent which always made me grin and which earned her a very half-hearted slap on her bare bottom.

'Physical abuse now, is it? Don't forget, mate, I could probably break you in half with my little finger,' she continued in the same accent,' which made me laugh out loud.

'OK. OK. I surrender,' I said now, remembering from a couple of our past adventures together how true that was.

'That's better,' she mumbled before finally falling asleep.

I lay there with the whole scenario with the Virago going through my mind but finally managed to fall asleep myself with no interruptions, thank God.

CHAPTER 20

FRIDAY

The next morning I got up early, feeling a bit groggy but putting it down either to the remains of jet lag or the bump on my head. I did all my bathroom stuff, then got dressed in my old comfortable clothes, made a large pot of coffee and drank it all down swiftly which revivified me, and finally got to unpack my bag properly. I put my pistol in my belt, thinking that I might be able to use it to intimidate Alexei. Then I put my notes, which I still hadn't been able to update properly, in my small document bag and, leaving a note for Pamela who hadn't resurfaced yet to tell her I'd had to go into the office, closed the door quietly behind me as I left and made my way down to where I'd left the car.

I drove slowly and carefully to the office, thinking the whole way about how I was going to get through to Alexei, and finally decided that the truth was probably the best policy. But, before I saw him, I knew I had to update Sir M properly and his office was my first stop. I looked at my watch and saw it was only just after 9am.

'All hail!' he said jovially when I went in. 'I didn't

expect you for a while yet so congratulations on that and also on the success of your mission of course. The PM is delighted with the outcome.'

'Good,' I said, 'although it certainly wasn't all plain sailing by any manner of means if I may use a very bad pun.'

'No, I'm aware of that but you got the result we all wanted, didn't you?'

'Yes, I suppose so but, as I told the President yesterday, it was very much a team effort. Without the total support of the carrier it would almost certainly have been a complete disaster.'

'Oh, so you've spoken to him?'

'Yes, just before I rang you. Anyway, the reason you are my first stop is because I want to bring you more up to date with what actually happened which I didn't have time to do yesterday.'

'I'm all ears, my boy,' he said.

So I did exactly that, filling in all the gaps in my narrative of the day before, especially the words we exchanged with the terrorists and my interpretation of their responses, minimal though they had been. Then I went on to describe the firestorm on the Virago and its breakup and the incredible scene of the missile exploding way up high. I skimmed over the death of the SEAL as I thought I might get too emotional if I went into it in any detail. I finished by telling him what I thought our political masters should say about the disappearance of a cable laying ship in the middle of the Atlantic.

He listened to me without interrupting but, as usual,

making a few notes on a pad in front of him, and, when I finally ground to a halt, he said, 'Yes, well, that all seems fair enough and, actually, I just have one question for you: Did you get checked over on the carrier for radiation poisoning? After all, it seems you were pretty close to where the missile on the ship exploded.'

I paused before replying, 'Now that was something I'd never considered. No I didn't. Do you think I ought to?'

'Yes, definitely,' came his swift reply, 'and sooner rather than later.'

'OK. Will do,' I said. 'Where do you think I could get it done? I hope I won't have to drive to Porton Down.'

'No, certainly not. Any of the big London teaching hospitals could do it. I'll make an appointment for you later in the day at St Thomas' if I can and if you want me to.'

'Thank you very much, Sir,' I said. And that was pretty much the end of the interview. I left him thinking morosely about the additional problem he'd given me. I didn't fancy the idea of getting radiation poisoning at all. But I knew I had to put that behind me for now and concentrate on this Russian wretch. However, first, I needed to see Alan and find out what he had to say about the prisoner, knowing he'd probably have even more up to date information about him than Sir M.

I tracked him down easily and, once we were both seated in my office and had done with all the usual congratulatory bullshit, asked him directly how our prisoner was. 'A little too perky for my liking, to be honest, boss. Considering the mess he's in physically. He's still insisting on speaking to someone at his Consulate and on his rights as a diplomat.'

'Well, I hope I can get through to him, that's all,' I said. 'Can you take me down to him now?'

'Sure. Give me a couple of minutes to set it up. Do you want any of the team to be present?'

'No, I don't think so. Let's keep the audience reasonably small, just you and the techies, to start with, anyway.'

'Yes, sir. Actually I've deputed Gloria and Ben to work the recording equipment. I thought that way there'd be less possibility of a potential leak.'

'Good thinking, Alan. I hadn't thought of that.' After he'd set everything up using the phone in my office, I followed him down to the basement where we kept the hardest criminals and terrorists and there, through the one-way mirror, got my first glimpse of the man who had, almost definitely, set up the whole obscene operation. I greeted Gloria and Ben in the big operations room with all the recording equipment and had to undergo the usual big welcome and congratulations. 'How's he been behaving?' I asked them.

'Like a lamb to the slaughter,' they replied or words to that effect.

'Anything else I need to know about him?'

'How about the other names on his bank accounts?' Gloria said.

'Yes, they might be very helpful. Thanks, Gloria.' And she passed me a bit of paper with three names on it, all English, I noted.

He was certainly a bit of a mess, not the dandy I'd

heard about all those days ago. His tie had been removed along with his belt and shoe laces and his suit, even if it was clearly once very expensive, was now very rumpled. I also noticed that his hair, which he was obviously very proud of, was now very mussed although he'd made an attempt to flatten it down with water. He was just sitting at a small table in his tiny cell, which had only a couple of hard upright chairs fixed to the floor and a sink and a toilet in the corner, with his feet manacled together but I also noticed he still had a strong gleam in his eyes and looked very alert. Maybe that would be helpful. I borrowed a packet of cigarettes from Alan and then went outside, round to his door, which I opened with my own pass.

I walked straight in and said, 'Mr Georgiev or should it be Mr Kandinsky?' I didn't wait for an answer but I noticed him straighten up immediately, and then continued, 'Or can I call you Alexei or Petrov? Which do you prefer?' and now I waited for an answer.

He eyed me up and down, took in the shabby state of my clothes, and said, 'I demand to speak to your boss.'

'I'm sorry about that but I'm afraid I am the boss around here. And I would say you're not in a position to make demands of me, wouldn't you?'

'Where am I?' he asked now.

'You're in one of the most secure locations in the country. Don't worry about that. Now what am I going to call you? We're not going to get very far if I don't even have a decent name for you.'

'You can call me Petrov as you seem to know

everything about me already,' he said sulkily now. 'What's your name?'

'You can call me Jack. So now we're on first name terms, Petrov, do you want to know why you're here? Would you like a cigarette, by the way?'

'No, thanks. I don't smoke. And yes, I would very much like to know what the hell I'm doing here and I also want to know why I haven't been given any access to my consulate or even allowed a phone call.'

'To answer your second two questions first, it's because I instructed my staff not to allow you access to anyone or anything until I got back from my travels. Now, as to your first question, I've been a busy bee foiling your plot to drop nuclear weapons on my country and America with a view to paralysing our electricity grids.' Now I saw him blanche and heard him whisper something to himself. 'Did you say I couldn't have done? I'm very much afraid that I did, with quite a bit of help from the Americans actually. Sorry about that, old son. Your ship, the Virago, is now lying at the bottom of the Atlantic along with its two medium range nuclear missiles.'

And now he crumpled and I thought he might just burst into tears. But his natural strength and dignity quickly reasserted itself and he asked very quietly, 'What do you want from me?'

'Now we're getting somewhere. That's a very good question. And it seems to me you have four options, Petrov. The first and probably simplest is for me to shoot you here and now.' And now I took out my pistol and laid it on the table between us, 'for which I am quite sure I will be applauded long and loud by those in the know about your little operation. There are any number of places where we could bury you and where you'd never be found.' And now I stopped.

Petrov thought about this for a second or two then, much to my relief, must have decided he didn't like it because he asked eagerly, 'And what are the other three options?'

'Option number two is to simply put you on a plane back to Moscow, without any of your remaining English assets, which have, by the way, all been frozen, including the ones in your English names, where you would doubtless have to explain to Vladimir where all the millions he spent on the operation have gone and how they've been totally wasted. I wonder if even you could talk your way out of that one and also if, perhaps, he's already told you to succeed or if you fail, to fall on your sword. Doubtless he will not be a very happy bunny and I suspect, knowing him, he will promptly have you executed.' And I watched for a reaction and saw him flinch. So I knew my little fishing expedition had hit the mark.

'And what's the third option?' he asked, thoroughly chastened now.

'The third option is to try you in camera in the courts where you are guaranteed to be convicted. The judge will certainly put you away for ever in one of our maximum security prisons and throw away the keys where you will probably be buggered to kingdom come by the other inmates, a pretty man like you, that is if you are ever let out of solitary confinement and where you will not be allowed any access at all to communications equipment of any kind.'

He winced at my colourful language and asked now, 'And the fourth option?'

'This is probably the best all round for you. It involves you being set free by us, given a new identity, a place to live, and a small sinecure. In return, of course, for talking to us about your past operations, which are probably all old hat anyway, and possibly a few other things as well. I realise of course that you'd be living under the constant threat of being murdered by your old pals in the GRU but I can absolutely assure you that we'd do everything in our power to not let that happen. And we have a pretty good reputation with our Witness Protection Programme, provided that you follow the rules.' And there I stopped. I could practically hear the cogs turning in his brain and I just hoped I had the measure of the man.

I waited a short while and then said, 'So what's it to be, Petrov?'

'And you yourself actually have the power to do any of these things? Is that true?'

'You'd better believe it,' I said as forcefully as I could.

'You know you're asking me to turn traitor?'

'Look on it as saving your miserable hide,' I said now. Then I got up from my chair and said, 'You can sleep on it if you want. I'll come back at the same time tomorrow but I'll need a definitive answer by then.' Then I just left the room, after picking up my pistol from the table, and I went next door to see how the recording had gone. It had apparently all come out beautifully. So I thanked Gloria and Ben and Alan and I went back up to my office where we sat down in our comfortable chairs.

'So how do you think that went?' I asked him.

'Pretty well, I thought. It was clever of you to bludgeon him with the truth. I have just one question, though: why did you allow him the day's grace to think about it?'

'I remembered you calling him a dandy or something like that soon after you first saw him. I've met people like him before and one thing I know about them is that they have a very strong sense of self-preservation. And I'm hoping that he will use that clever brain of his to see that he really is between the devil and the deep, blue sea and will understand that 'turning traitor', as he put it, is really the only option for him. I'd much rather he worked that out for himself than being put under a lot of pressure to decide at once. It's a bit risky, I know, but I'd say the odds were in our favour.'

'Yes, I understand now.'

'Good. Now to practicalities: first, does he have family in Russia?' I could see Alan trying to remember, a bit thrown by the abrupt change of subject.

'Now you mention it, boss, I think he's got a wife but they're not close, according to Toby, but no kids as far as I'm aware. Why do you want to know?'

'Simply because, from my experience of other defectors, they usually ask if we could bring members of their families over, if they're going to cooperate with us, and that, almost always, involves complications, especially with someone as obviously important as he is.'

'Oh, OK. I understand now. I will of course check that with Toby.'

'Thanks, sooner rather than later, please, with details of names etc. if he knows them. And the second thing is: Can you please draw up an official, legal form for the Witness Protection Programme, guaranteeing that we will actually abide by my promises? You can ask any of the team for help if you need it. I will take it round to the PM myself or the Home secretary later if I have to. I think he will almost certainly ask for something like that if he's going to go ahead with it. I know I would and I'd rather be prepared.'

'Yes, boss, consider it done.'

'Thanks, Alan. Now I suppose I'm going to have to go up to Sir M and convince him that what I've done is in the best interests of the country although I don't think he'll need much convincing.' After he'd left to run my errands, I looked at my watch and saw it was already 12.10. Where has the morning gone? I asked myself. But then I realised I was hungry and decided to put off Sir M until after I'd eaten. So I went up to the executive canteen and ate a good lunch.

After that, it was definitely time to brief Sir M so up I went to the top floor and, after being waved through by his dragon lady of a secretary, went into his office where I found him still drowning in my files.

'Hello, Jack, come to save me from all your paperwork at last?' he boomed in greeting.

'Not yet, I'm afraid, Sir M. Actually I've come to update you on my interview with the slippery Alexei.'

'Oh, yes, I'd forgotten about him momentarily. I'm all ears. Fire away.'

So I told him what had transpired down in the basement as exactly as I could remember it and, when I told him about the last option I'd presented to him, he whistled and said, 'You cheeky bugger! I never thought you'd be able to turn him so easily.'

'Just a question of reading his character, Sir. And, of course, it's not a done deal yet. I've given him a day to think about it.'

'Very kind of you, Jack, but I presume you're optimistic about the outcome?'

'Yes, reasonably, if I've read him right, that is.'

Then I went on to tell him what I'd asked Alan to do and he said that both of the things sounded like sensible precautions. I finished by saying that, if he became a defector, he would probably, according to Toby, be the highest-ranking one we'd ever managed to get.

'Yes, I'm aware of that. Well done, Jack, on progress so far. Keep me informed.' And that was the end of that particular interview.

I went back to my office, wondering whether I'd done the right thing, but decided, on balance, that I had. Then I met my secretary who was agog for news but I had to tell her the whole thing was still under wraps and probably would be for the foreseeable future which disappointed her. However, I managed to placate her by saying that it would probably all be over by the next day and then everything would be back to normal. I knew that now I just had to sit around and wait for Alan to contact me so I decided to update my notes.

I finished doing that about 3 pm, still not having heard from Alan, and I thought that a quick phone call from me to him wouldn't hurt so I rang him.

'Sorry I didn't get back to you sooner, boss, but I've been all wrapped up in the red tape involved in getting one of these blasted documents. But I think I'm nearly there now. Give me another hour, OK?'

'That's fine. What about his family connections?'

'Oh, yes. Sorry again. It completely slipped my mind that you wanted to know urgently. I spoke to Toby as soon as I left you and he confirmed that he was an only child with both parents dead, a wife he apparently only sees very rarely and no kids. Apparently again, he regards Medvedev as a sort of substitute father.'

'That's rather sad but is very good news for us. It means he's a real loner and has no reason for asking anyone to join him here.'

'Yes, I guess so.'

'Who do you have to get to sign the infernal document?'

'Either the PM or the Home Secretary.'

'Would you mind taking it to Sir M when you've got it? I know for a fact that the Home Secretary is rather scared of us lot and, if Sir M himself turned up on her doorstep and asked her to sign it, I'm sure she would without asking too many awkward questions. I'll ring him now and prepare him.'

'Sure thing, boss.'

'Thanks, Alan,' and we disconnected. Then I rang Sir M and prepared him for Alan's visit and gave him my reasons.

He grunted and said, 'Yes, OK, Jack,' adding humorously, 'your wish is my command but you can't be forever having me run around doing your bidding. I expect she's in town near the centre of the action and it's not yet the Parliamentary recess.'

'I hope this will be the last time for a while, Sir, but thanks anyway.'

He grunted again and hung up.

I clapped my hands in glee as it meant I could now go home with nothing else absolutely urgent on my plate. So that's what I did to my usual rapturously amusing wife who said, 'Have you still got a job, Jack? If so, what are you doing back so early? I could have been up to absolutely anything.'

'Yes, actually, I do. But I'm still feeling the effects of jet lag and needed another early night.'

'Poor old man, you. As long as it's not too early, that's fine,' and she gave me one of her lecherous winks which she knew always turned me on. 'Do you want supper early then?'

'Actually, I was thinking of taking you out somewhere. Where would you like to go?'

'That's a great idea. Are we celebrating something?'

'No, not really. Just thought it might be nice for you.'

'OK. How about our lovely Italian trattoria?'

'Sure. I'll book a table. I know it's Friday but we

must be two of the owner's best clients and it shouldn't be difficult.'

'Yes, you do that while I go and get tarted up a bit.'

So we did that and had our usual lovely meal there, being greeted like long-lost best friends and both of us being kissed on both cheeks by the padrone. We talked during the meal about everything and nothing and then wobbled a bit tipsily home and into bed. It was time for hanky-panky and finally sleep.

CHAPTER 21

SATURDAY

I woke up in a panic in the middle of the night, having remembered what I'd promised I'd do for Sir M: get myself tested for radiation poisoning. Oh well, there was always today, I supposed, but I'd probably have to grovel to him and to the hospital. I remembered also that I'd turned off my phone, not wanting to be disturbed. Silly of me but never mind and I finally managed to go back to sleep.

When I woke up the next morning, for some unknown reason I felt optimistic about how the day would pan out and I was actually whistling when I put the coffee on. I looked to see if I had any messages on my mobile and, indeed, there were two, the first from Sir M to say that he hadn't managed to get an appointment for the hospital yesterday but instead had done so for today at 3pm, telling me the name of the doctor it'd be with. So that was OK. The second was from Alan to say that he'd passed the document on to Sir M to take to the Home Secretary. It was timed at 4.15pm so I hoped he'd managed to do it. There would seem to have been plenty of time but Sir M hadn't got back to me, which was a bit of a worry, and I decided to try him on his mobile.

He answered at once. 'Hello, Jack. Nice of you to call an old man. Why did you turn off your phone yesterday? I do hope you're not going to make a habit of that.'

'Because I decided to go home early and I didn't want to be disturbed. And no, I'm not going to make a habit of it,' I told him truthfully.

'Hmm. OK. I can't say I blame you. If I had someone like your delectable Pamela to go home to, I probably would have done the same.'

I smiled to myself, thinking of the procession of young, luscious housekeepers I'd met at his house over the years. But I knew this was business and I turned right to it, asking him if he'd managed to take the document round to the Home Secretary for signing.

'Of course, my boy. It was all very straightforward. It's now sitting on my desk, waiting for you to collect it.'

'Good news. Thank you very much indeed for sorting that out, Sir.'

'My pleasure, Jack. I'm on my way into the office as I speak. When can I expect the pleasure of your company?'

'I'm leaving here in a few minutes, Sir.'

'Good. See you soon,' and he hung up.

So everything seemed to be going my way. Maybe I had reason to be optimistic. I drank my coffee quickly, left a short note for Pamela, and went down to my car. I drove to the office, thinking about possible changes of plan if Petrov didn't end up liking my final option. I'd deliberately left my pistol at home today as I didn't think I could shoot another professional in cold blood.

When I got there, I went straight up to Sir M's office and retrieved my document. I took it down to my own office and perused it carefully. It was certainly impressive, decorated with all kinds of seals and the Home Secretary's signature in bold writing at the end and it seemed to say all the right things, right down to the possibility of plastic surgery if he wanted to change his appearance, and I was pleased with Alan's diligence. It was now about 9.15. So I had just over an hour to kill and I thought I could most fruitfully spend the time having a proper breakfast as I'd only had coffee so far. So I went to the executive canteen and had a full English which probably didn't do much for my carbohydrate levels but certainly improved the clarity of my thinking processes as eating usually did for me. Then it was back to my own office again where I rang Alan and congratulated him on the clarity of the document and asked him if everything was set up.

He told me it was so I went on down to the basement with its overall sense of hopelessness (which, by the way, was absolutely deliberate) and met up with him there in the recording studio next door to Petrov's cell. Gloria and Ben were already there testing the equipment and I had the opportunity to study the prisoner again through the one-way mirror. He still looked reasonably alert although even more dishevelled than yesterday and I knew in my gut how much he must be wanting a decent shower and change of clothes.

'OK, guys. Let's get this over with,' I said and walked out of the studio and opened the door to his cell, carrying the precious document. 'Hi, Petrov! How are you feeling today?'

'I've been thinking about your options,' he said surlily.

'Do go on. And what have you decided?'

'I don't really have much choice, do I?'

'I think that about sums it up, yes.'

'I think I'll have to turn traitor against my own country, God help me. I know I wouldn't survive five minutes in one of your prisons and I certainly can't go back to mother Russia now as you quite correctly pointed out yesterday.' Now he paused briefly before continuing, 'However, I would need some kind of guarantee of my safety and that you actually have the power to do everything you said.'

'Do you mean something like this?' I said, passing him the document, my heart leaping.

He sat back and read it through very carefully from beginning to end, going over each sentence twice to make absolutely sure he hadn't missed anything. It took him about 15 minutes but I would have given him as much time as he wanted. Meanwhile I just sat there and waited. When he'd finished, he uttered a Russian swearword which I knew from my time in his country and said, 'Is this for real?'

'As real as it gets,' I replied.

'How did you know I'd ask for this?'

'It wasn't difficult. Just a question of knowing what

kind of person you were. I guessed you really didn't want to die.'

'Very clever of you,' he admitted grudgingly.

'I'm quite sure you've made the right decision, Petrov.'

'Hmm. I wonder.'

'Now we just need your signature at the end, please,' and I passed him a pen.

He scribbled something on the document and I took it back from him and checked that he hadn't signed 'Mickey Mouse' or something but no, it said perfectly clearly 'Petrov Kandinsky.' He was clearly a decisive man who could make decisions for himself very quickly.

'Thank you,' I said. 'Perhaps now you'd like to think of an English name for yourself, where you might like to live and what your legend should be. I would suggest somewhere like an English market town, not too big, and something like an investment banker who's retired to the country. I'll leave you alone now for a while to get used to being an English gentleman and tell your guards to bring you a change of clothing and let you have a decent shower. I'm afraid, however, you'll be a guest here for a bit longer while we start your debriefing.' I carefully avoided the word 'interrogation'.

'How long are you talking about?'

'Just until you've given us enough concrete proof that you're now on our side. I'm sure you can appreciate that it's got to be a two-way street from now on.'

'Yes, I suppose so,' he said rather disconsolately. 'Well, I suppose also I need to say thank you to you, Jack, for saving my miserable hide as you so poetically put it yesterday.'

I grinned at this, surprised that he seemed to have a sense of humour, which he hadn't shown any sign of until now, and he managed a wry grin back. 'Your English is really very good, Petrov.' He preened a little at my words and I sincerely hoped he wouldn't pose any more problems. On the whole, I didn't think so. He knew how easy it would be for us to throw him back into the shark-infested sea of his old world if we wanted. Of course he would try to obfuscate as much as possible but all professional interrogators knew how to deal with that and we had some of the best in the world, I believed. I knew every aspect of his past life would be taken apart and examined microscopically for the truth. And it was with these thoughts going through my head that I left him alone.

I went back to the recording studio to a round of applause from the three of them inside and asked Gloria and Ben how the recording had gone. 'As clear as a bell,' they told me.

'Good because that tape could be very important in the future if we ever have to throw him to the wolves. I reckon it's pretty good leverage, don't you, guys?'

'Absolutely, sir,' they said. 'We'll make several copies of it now.'

'Thanks, chaps. I think I'll just wait here while you do that as I'm sure Sir M will be interested to hear it and possibly also the PM.' It didn't take them long and, as soon as I had my copies, I bade them farewell and told them we'd have one more meeting of the whole team, possibly the next day. I knew that was important as they'd probably have many questions for me, which I knew deserved answers.

Then I took the precious tape up to Sir M and played it through to him. 'Well,' he said after it had finished, 'you seem to have read his character all right after all, Jack. Congratulations. I think I might just take this round to the PM.'

'Yes, Sir. I thought you might want to do that.'

'Now can I please give you back your files?'

'Yes, I suppose so although I was hoping for a day or two's grace. Remember I'm supposed to be going for a radiation check-up this afternoon.'

'Oh, yes, so you are. OK. How does 24 hours grab you?'

'And I also have to tell the team what's been happening. They've been pretty much left in the dark since I left for my seafaring trip.'

'You're a hard bargainer, Jack, but OK. I'll give you 48 hours but not a second longer.'

'Thank you very much, Sir.' And on that note I left him, almost skipping with joy. I went back to my office and wondered how I was going to spend the next few hours until my appointment. My watch said 11.30, too early for lunch. Then I had an idea. I'd been completely out of touch with the news recently and I wanted to catch up, especially to see if anybody had caught the story about what had happened in the mid-Atlantic. So I asked my secretary, who was in today on hand to help Sir M if needed, to bring me up from our Periodicals and

Newspapers department copies of all the broadsheets from the past couple of days and, meanwhile, I turned on my computer and Googled BBC news, asking for any stories about the mid-Atlantic. And there was one about a very bright light in the sky which had been seen by several ships but it was explained away as either a large meteorite burning up in the atmosphere or an old spacecraft doing the same, probably the latter. There was absolutely nothing about the Virago and I thought we'd been lucky it had been sunk in such an empty part of the ocean. Then my secretary appeared with the few newspapers which still bothered with printing on paper (much my own preferred format) and not simply downloading all their stories online. But by then it was 12.20 and I felt I deserved some lunch so I went back to the Executive canteen and ate alone as usual.

After that I perused all the papers, focussing particularly on any stories with a terrorist connection which might come back to bite me later. But I skimmed everything, knowing that I needed to be up with politics and everything else if I was to be able to do my job properly. Fortunately, however, there wasn't much hard news (it was the start of the silly season after all), the usual scandals about celebrities and politicians getting up to mischief but nothing that would impinge on my job, I hoped.

I looked at my watch again and saw it was now 2.15, time to start heading off to the hospital so I called reception and asked them to book me a taxi. To be perfectly honest, I was scared witless of hospitals myself although I had been in them many times on behalf of others, especially my first wife who had finally died of cancer in one. But to the best of my recollection, I hadn't been in hospital myself since I was a child. I'd always been in rude health. So it was with some trepidation that I made my way to St Thomas' and presented myself at reception.

'I believe I have an appointment to see a Doctor Kalgan at 3pm about possible radiation poisoning,' I said hesitantly.

'What's your name, sir?' the receptionist said reasonably.

'Mr Jack Sanderson.'

'Oh, yes, here you are. You're a private patient, I understand?'

'I'm not sure. Sorry. The appointment was organised by my boss, Sir Maurice – er - Oldham. He took care of everything.' I had to think for a microsecond about Sir M's surname as I used it so rarely.

'Yes, that's right. You'll need to go to radiology,' she said and gave me directions. I thanked her and left her desk.

Then it was just a simple matter of getting lost a couple of times before I found it. I thought I might be back on the aircraft carrier the place was so huge. But find it I did and I presented myself to another receptionist who told me to wait in the reception area and said the doctor would be along shortly. I wondered whether Sir M even knew that a National Health Service existed – an amusing speculation that kept me occupied for the very short time I had to wait. Then a suave-looking gentleman came in, who reminded me a bit of Alexei in his better days, and said, 'Mr Jack Sanderson?' I got up and followed him down yet another corridor to a smallish but reasonably comfortable office.

We went in and he sat behind a big desk, gesturing to me to sit in the chair facing him. 'Now tell me what happened,' he said. 'Why do you think you might have been exposed to radiation?'

This was a turn up for the books. I knew I couldn't tell him the whole truth but neither could I lie. 'I think I might have been near an exploding nuclear missile,' I said uncomfortably.

'And, let me guess, you can't tell me any more than that?' he said now, seemingly unperturbed by my bizarre confession, and I just nodded miserably. 'I hope, however, you can tell me when this event occurred?'

I had to do a quick calculation in my head, so much had happened recently. 'About three days ago,' I said, 'although it was in a different time zone.'

'OK. Well, if you were exposed, we should be able to treat you then. First, however, have you had any nausea or vomiting?'

'No, none at all.' I didn't bother telling him about the rough sea crossing I'd had to make when the blue pill I'd been given by Chuck seemed to have done its work of preventing me from getting sea sick.

'Good. That means that it's very unlikely that you've been exposed to a large dose.' I saw him making notes of my answers on a long form and he went on to ask many more questions about symptoms, to all of which I replied in the negative, including one about whether I was more forgetful than usual, which I found interesting. I must admit that he was very thorough although I was surprised that he didn't carry out any kind of physical examination and I asked him about this. He told me that the symptoms always told him enough to be able to diagnose whether a patient has radiation sickness although he had to rely on him or her telling the truth. 'I think I can say with total confidence that, if you were exposed, the amount of exposure was negligible. However, that said, if you do get any unexplained fits of vomiting or nausea in the next couple of weeks, I hope you will not hesitate to come back and see me again.'

'That's a big relief, Doctor. Yes, of course I will. It's good to know I won't be glowing in the dark.'

'My patients always say that and my standard response is, if you do start glowing in the dark, I'd be very interested to hear about it.' And now he grinned at me and I grinned back. 'The other question they usually ask is, why haven't I been scanned with a Geiger counter? And my standard response again is because Geiger counters are only useful to measure radiation levels at a particular location and are no use at all at diagnosing radiation sickness later on in the human body. The other thing to bear in mind is that different individuals react differently to radiation poisoning, although the nausea and vomiting seem to be a constant, but it's perfectly possible that you have a decent genome which doesn't react too unfavourably to a small dose of radiation.

I hope that answers all your questions.' And now he stopped.

'Yes, indeed, Doctor. And again thank you very much indeed for your reassurance. Do I owe you anything?'

'No. It's all been taken care of by Sir Maurice.' And that was that. I left him with a much lighter heart than on my arrival and found my way out of the labyrinth – eventually. There I got another taxi back to the office where I rang up to Sir M to give him the news.

'Good, Jack. I hope you feel it was worth going however. You seem to have the valuable knack of always landing on your feet.'

I didn't know what to say to this so I just told him I was leaving to go home now but I'd leave my mobile switched on this time in case there were any emergencies, to which he just grunted. Then I rang Alan and told him also that I was leaving now but to assemble the team for the next morning at 10 am. After that it was just a question of telling my secretary that I was off and giving Pamela a quick call and I was free to go! It was now 5pm on a Saturday so I didn't feel guilty in the slightest.

I drove home slowly thinking about Sir M's final words and finally decided that yes, I was a bloody lucky old sod. There I had my usual lovely supper and after doing the washing up, watched a bit of mindless TV and finally went to bed, tired after yet another eventful day.

CHAPTER 22

SUNDAY

I got up the next morning at 6.15 as usual, pottered around a bit, read the paper and then made breakfast for Pamela and myself. She was up by this time and we ate together as usual at the weekend. I told her I had to go into the office that morning and she accepted this without complaining. Then I went down to the garage, collected my car and drove easily to work as there wasn't that much traffic, arriving about 9.15. Once there, I immediately rang Toby from my office, feeling a bit guilty as I hadn't kept him in the loop about Petrov. He was delighted to hear that the Russian was now a bona fide defector and immediately asked when he'd be able to talk to him.

'Sooner rather than later,' I replied, knowing that my guys wanted to have first bite of the cherry. 'But don't worry. We'll soften him up for you.'

'Thanks. Don't forget now.'

'Oh, I won't, I promise.'

'And don't forget that the Americans will want to talk to him too.'

'Well, they'll just have to wait in line, won't they?' I said. And that was pretty much the end of that conversation. I looked at my watch again and it was now about 9.45 so I rang Alan and asked him if everyone was now in the building as I thought we might as well start early if that was the case.

'I'll just check,' he said and I waited while he did that. 'Yes, everyone is here now,' he told me.

'Good. Why don't we start soon then? I'll make my way to the conference room.'

'OK, boss,' he replied.

When I got there, Alan was already there and the others were slowly trickling in. As soon as we were all present and correct, I started by saying, 'Sorry to have called you all in on a Sunday but I thought it might be a good idea to give you the chance to question me about what's been happening since I left for the carrier. Then, hopefully, we can wrap up this whole affair. First, however, I hope you've all now been informed that your man, Alexei, or Petrov as I prefer to call him now, has decided to come over to us.' Now I paused and they all nodded.

Dennis took it upon himself to speak for all of them by saying, 'We'd all like to congratulate you, sir, on a job well done there.'

'Thank you for that, Dennis. So can we move on? I, for one, am hoping to be home by lunchtime. I leave the floor to you all to ask any questions you like.' There was a short pause while they thought, followed quickly by a flurry of questions, mainly dealing with the action against the Virago. I answered them all totally honestly, not mincing my words, and I could see how well this went down.

Lucy, however, managed to touch a nerve when she said, 'You must have been very upset when you found out you'd lost a SEAL, weren't you?'

But I still managed to answer truthfully, 'Yes, I was. Very.'

Then Felicity asked, 'What was the scariest moment for you?' and I had to think before answering. But I told her that it was probably when we were speeding away from the ship and were hit by the massive tsunami and I thought we were going to overturn. And this initiated a whole lot more questions since I hadn't mentioned it before. I caught myself rubbing the back of my head while I was answering them, subconsciously, I think. But they finally ran out of questions and I found myself sweating a lot, having remembered the whole thing in detail.

Now Alan spoke up. 'On behalf of all of us, I'd like to thank you, sir, for giving us this opportunity to question you. It's obviously taken a lot out of you.' And there was a big round of applause at his words.

'Thank you, Alan, for your kind words. Now go home and enjoy the rest of the weekend,' I said in parting. 'See you all tomorrow, I trust.' And they all filed out, quite sobered by what I'd told them.

I still had one more thing to do now: see how Petrov was getting on. So I went down to the basement where I opened the door to his cell. I found him surrounded by bits of paper on which he'd scribbled several signatures with a pencil he was holding. He was looking much better now, I thought, obviously having bathed and changed into some of his own clothes which had been brought over from his flat: a nicely cut pair of jeans with an expensive-looking gabardine shirt and some decent slip-on shoes, I noticed. His hair was all back in place too, having been washed and combed. He wasn't manacled any more either, which pleased me until I remembered that nobody had known I was coming.

'So I hope you're feeling better today, Petrov?' I said by way of greeting.

'Yes, much better, thanks. I guess it's you I have to thank for all this?' he said, waving at his clothes and the pencil and papers. 'But I'm really looking forward to getting out of here.'

'I reckon you might have to wait another week or so. Sorry about that but it takes a while to sort everything out. Have you decided on a name yet that you like?' I said, gesturing at the signatures.

'I think so but I'm not 100% sure yet.'

'That's OK. But let the debriefers know as soon as you've decided, won't you? I imagine they'll be starting tomorrow.'

'What day of the week is it?' he asked now and I remembered how easy it was to get disorientated if you were totally cut off from the outside world.

'It's Sunday, actually. So not long to wait.'

'Can I have some newspapers, do you think? And maybe a chess set?'

'Yes, I don't see why not. I'll tell your guards on my way out.'

'Thank you, Jack. My cup overfloweth.' And there it was again- a flash of humour. 'I can't wait to get started actually.'

'Good. That's the spirit. Well, I'll leave you now. Be good.' And I smiled at him.

'Not much chance of anything else, is there?' he said, grinning. I grinned back at him, waved him goodbye and left, not forgetting to tell his guards to bring him whatever English papers he wanted and a chess set on the way out.

He'd reminded me of one more thing I needed to do: to make sure that our two best interrogators were actually available for Monday. So back in my office again I rang Alan and asked him and he reassured me that indeed they were and were even now doing their homework on Petrov, having been given everything we knew about him. I thanked him very much for his proactive approach to this, which had completely slipped my mind.

'It's all part of my job, sir – to watch your back.'

'Can you ask them when they turn up to come and see me briefly? I'd like to give them a few pointers.'

'Sure thing, boss. I'm sure they'll be delighted with all the help they can get.'

'Thanks again.' And I disconnected.

After that I just went home and got there in time to take Pamela out to a local pub for a nice lunch. We went for our usual walk on Hampstead Heath after we'd eaten and then back home and spent what remained of the weekend relaxing, like I imagined normal couples do.

CHAPTER 23

THE AFTERMATH

I went in on Monday morning to find Bill and Ben (our names for our two most experienced interrogators) waiting for me. I ushered them straight into my office and didn't beat about the bush.

'Petrov is not your usual defector,' I said. 'Indeed, he is very special indeed as I'm sure you've gathered from reading his file. So if I may suggest you treat him with kid gloves and all due deference. His English is superb so you have nothing to worry about there and, as you've probably been told, I have personally guaranteed him safe sanctuary in this country if he cooperates fully with you guys. I have also promised him that he will be moved to a safe house by the end of the week so you'll have to get your skates on if you're going to be able to ok that. I suggest you simply take him through his CV to start with before you ask him any potentially awkward questions about reasonably current operations he's been involved in. I see no reason why he shouldn't cooperate but there's a lot riding on you guys as he's probably the most important defector we've ever had. I'm hoping that eventually he will be able to give us the Kremlin's strategic thinking which will be absolutely invaluable.' And there I stopped, hoping that my seriousness had got through to both of them. They both nodded emphatically and I asked finally if they had any questions for me but they didn't so I dismissed them to get on with their work but not before asking them to keep me updated on a daily basis.

Then it was simply a question of retrieving my files from Sir M and getting back into the swing of my normal routine. There were, however, a few more loose ends to sort out before I could put the whole affair behind me. The first was, how in hell's name did the terrorists manage to transfer the missiles to the Virago? I could just ask Petrov but he might see that as weakness and I didn't want that. I was, after all, supposed to be omniscient. And for an answer I knew I had to turn to Toby. So I rang him and asked and he said that his team suspected strongly an Abu Dhabi-registered freighter which passed near the Virago about six weeks before we got onto them. They could easily have transferred them at night but, frustratingly, he had no hard proof of it as the freighter was now crossing the Pacific on its way back to Abu Dhabi where it would be untouchable. But he agreed with me that it would have been impossible to bring the missiles into Britain and load them in Liverpool. So that was one unresolved mystery.

Another was: what were the real identities of the terrorists on board? And I asked Toby that too. He said that they had been researching that also, in conjunction with the Americans, but they hadn't got far as the voice recognition software that they used wasn't sensitive enough to identify the voice with whom I'd communicated, given the short conversation I'd had with him, and we'd not had any visual contact.

'What about the officer in the picture?' I asked him now.

'That is interesting,' he said. 'Our facial recognition software came up with a 62% probability that it was somebody we've had dealings with in the Gulf before and who has been a thorn in our side for quite a while. He's quite senior in the Al Qaeda organisation and he seems to have dropped out of sight for the past few months. I just hope he didn't enter Britain illegally but was transferred from the freighter also at the same time as the missiles. That would seem to be the much more likely scenario.'

'Thank you very much indeed for all that, Toby. It certainly puts my own mind at rest. I presume you've passed all this on to our political masters?'

'I asked my boss to do that and I presume he's done it by now.'

'Anything else you can tell me?'

'No, I think that's it. You've asked the two pertinent questions we've been researching. I presume it's now back to the same old, same old for you?'

I groaned and said, 'Yes, indeed. But I owe you a large one, Toby. Thanks for all your help.'

'Any time, mate.' And there we both hung up.

The only other thing that happened in relation to the case occurred about a month later after Petrov had been tucked up in a safe house for a while and was singing like a bird. I got a phone call from the White House Chief of Staff, no less, who asked me if I could possibly come over on the Sunday two weeks from that day as the POTUS himself would very much like to meet me. I was gob-smacked by this as I'd completely forgotten his invitation to me but of course I said yes. He went on to say that they were sending me a first class return ticket and would put me up in a classy hotel for the night as it involved a dinner with him.

'Thank you very much,' was all I could find to say to this.

I thought about this invitation and decided that Sir M would surely give me a couple of days' leave. The only problem was Pamela. How on earth would I explain going to America to her (and without her)? Then I decided to simply tell a little of the truth without going into detail. That decision made, I now called Sir M and told him about the invitation.

'Well deserved, Jack, well deserved,' was pretty much all he said, except for agreeing that I could have two days' leave that week. Later, when I finished work and went home, I cornered Pamela in the kitchen.

'Pamela, I need to talk to you. Do you remember that case I was on just over a month ago which involved a trip to America? Well, I need to return there in a couple of weeks to finish off some final details with some colleagues over there and the trip will also probably involve a posh dinner. I'll only be gone about two or three days maximum as I'll need to get back to work.' I was quite pleased with my little speech, which I'd been rehearsing in the car, as I hadn't actually lied but had included all the important details.

She listened to me and said at once, 'How posh is posh?'

I wriggled uncomfortably at her question and replied, 'Very, I imagine.'

'OK,' she said now, 'we'll have to get you tarted up then, won't we? Don't worry. I'll see to your clothes.'

I breathed a sigh of relief that I seemed to have got away with it with no more questions from her. The next couple of weeks went by in a blur, my tickets arriving exactly as promised, and on the Saturday of that week I was driven to Heathrow by Pamela and waved goodbye to at the barrier. Then it was simply a question of going through security as I already had my boarding pass and had checked my bags in and then I was on the plane. I had forgotten how luxurious first class was on the big Jumbos and had an extremely comfortable flight, managing to sleep most of the way, avoiding all the free booze. We got to Washington airport on time and I was met there by a State department limo which whisked me off to a really lovely hotel, not far from the White House, which had views of its extensive grounds from every window. I even had my own suite on the top floor, which was beautifully appointed!

Then, after unpacking and hanging up my best suit carefully, I rang Pamela, told her everything was fine, ordered a very good meal from room service and a bit later crashed out on what was probably the most comfortable mattress I've ever slept on. I'd been told by the limo driver that I would be collected at 5pm the next day and taken to the White House, which would, I hoped, give me a little time for sightseeing. I'd been to Washington before of course but it wasn't a city I could claim to know well.

The next morning I got up late, having apparently recovered from any incipient jet lag, and determined after breakfast to go the Capitol building which I'd seen in so many movies and documentaries but had never been round. I knew I could have walked there as it really wasn't far but I wanted to ride in a proper Washington cab so I got the manager to order me one (all the staff seemed to want to fall over themselves to do my bidding) and it came quickly. Once there I got onto a regular tourist tour and spent a fascinating couple of hours just touring the building. That done, I went to look at the Washington memorial, another iconic landmark, and walked most of the way round the huge lake it fronted. It was very peaceful with just a few joggers. Then I thought I'd better go back to the hotel so I got another cab and, when I got there, went for a swim in its huge indoor pool. By this time I was hungry again so I went to the hotel restaurant and had a lightish meal, remembering the multitude of courses I'd had on my last visit to the White House with Pamela and not wanting to spoil my appetite.

After that it was back to my room where I had a long shower and got dressed very carefully, making sure not to wrinkle my best dry-cleaned suit. Then I just sat down and waited for my driver to arrive. Needless to say he did, on the dot of 5 pm (I'd remembered to change time zones on my watch this time!) and next it was off to meet the new POTUS. I remembered the previous one very well and what a nice guy he was and wondered how this one would measure up to him. I was met at the West Wing entrance by a flunky of some description who took me straight off to the Oval Office. I remembered this room very well also so I wasn't quite so overwhelmed with awe as I'd been the first time and, when the President turned out to be just as nice as the first one I'd met, I was overjoyed. He asked me straight out how my flight had been and how the hotel was and actually seemed to listen to my answers. After this, though, he turned to business and said forcefully, 'I can't tell you, Jack, how grateful this country is to you. Without your very positive intervention God knows where we'd be today.' I was embarrassed by this and told him how much of a team effort it had been and he said now without responding directly to my point, 'I have a bit of a surprise for you on that score but you're going to have to wait until dinner for it. Now I know my predecessor gave you the freedom of the country and the Congressional Medal of Honour and I've been racking my brains to think of what can possibly beat those and I finally came up with something much more personal which I hope you'll like. You'll find it waiting for you in your room at the hotel but please don't open it until you're on the plane home. OK?'

What could I say to this except just nod and say,

'Thank you very much indeed, sir. If it's appropriate, may I give it to my team back home?'

'Of course you may. It's yours to do with as you like.'

'Thank you once again, sir.'

'And now shall we go into dinner? I hope you're hungry.' And I nodded again, the force of his personality coming through every word.

And getting up from behind his desk, he actually took my elbow and it was like that that we made an entrance into the big dining room I remembered also from my previous trip, although it had now been redecorated. And what a surprise it was! There were a bunch of guys sitting around the huge table, all dressed in their very best dress uniforms, and I immediately recognised most of them from the carrier. There was my entire SEALS team there (minus Ryan of course) as well as the leader of the ABM unit although there were a couple of young Air Force pilots who I didn't know but presumed they were the fliers of the jets which had sunk the Virago. I immediately went up to Chuck and shook his hand vigorously saying, 'It's very good to see you, mate. But I must admit it's a bit of a shock.'

'He kept it under his hat, did he?' he said, gesturing at the President. But I didn't have time to respond as I was going around the table shaking everybody's hands. When I came to the Air Force pilots, I told them who I presumed they were, and they said yes, I was absolutely correct.

'It's very good to meet you at last,' I said. 'You did a fine job.'

'Thank you, sir,' one of them said while the other chipped in saying, 'It's very good to meet you too.'

'Let's eat now, shall we?' the President said once I'd been round the whole table, with a broad grin on his face. He'd obviously enjoyed surprising me. So we all sat down with me on the President's right and Chuck next to me, which I thought was a nice gesture. There were no women at all present, which, when I thought about it, didn't surprise me. It was clearly a meal designed especially for only those intimately connected with the operation.

I asked Chuck while the waiters were serving the first course if the Ohio was back in the US now and he told me that they'd got back just a few days before, which presumably accounted for the timing of the meal. Then I turned to the President and asked him where the Admiral was and he said that he was busy getting the carrier ready for its next mission. Then he added, 'I'm pleased that my little surprise seems to have worked.'

'Yes, indeed, sir. It's lovely to see all the lads again.'

However, then we started eating but between courses I asked Chuck first where Ryan had been buried. He said, 'Wisconsin in his home town. We usually bury them there rather than Arlington. It's more discreet.'

'Oh, OK,' I said remembering the passion for secrecy, even after death, the British Special Forces had and presuming it was exactly the same for the Americans. Then I asked what the medals were that I saw, pinned to all their uniforms, and he said that they were all gallantry medals. Apparently, they'd all been awarded them earlier that afternoon and I was pleased that the President had remembered his promise to reward all the guys involved. The meal went by in a blur but it was very good, needless to say. At one point, the President turned to me and whispered, 'It was good to hear you managed to turn the mastermind behind the operation into a defector. I hope you'll let us have a crack at him soon.'

'I'm sure that can be arranged, sir,' I said, surprised that he was so well informed. 'But I hope we're sharing any intelligence which concerns your interests. I haven't had time to follow up that end of things.'

'Yes, I believe you are although I don't think he's divulged anything really juicy yet.'

'Give him time, sir. I'm sure he will in the end,' I said. That was the end of the interesting things that were said at the meal and after I'd been around the table once more, wished them all luck on their next mission and said a warm farewell to the President, I found myself back in the limo and being whisked back to the hotel. There I found a large, quite heavy parcel with a Presidential seal on it but, remembering my promise to the POTUS, I didn't open it although I did wonder what it could possibly be. Then I rang Pamela and told her what time I should be getting back to Heathrow the next day and, after that, simply collapsed into bed, tired after all the day's excitement and knowing I'd have to get up quite early to catch my plane.

I was woken the next morning by my alarm and did all my morning stuff before staggering down to the restaurant for a decent breakfast. Then it was back to my room to pack and finally I was ready to leave the USA. The limo arrived, I was taken to the airport and soon found myself sitting in the plane as everything had gone with its usual smoothness although the security people did a double take when they X-rayed my package, which I was carrying as hand luggage, but the Presidential seal made them refrain from comment. I was, after all, flying first class! Then we were in the air and I opened the heavy parcel and got my second major surprise of my trip. After breaking the seal and ripping off the wrapping paper, I found a large walnut box, beautifully made, which contained a pair of silver-plated Smith and Wesson revolvers, nestling in their individual satin-lined containers, both of which had engraved on their handles, 'To Jack Sanderson. For services rendered,' followed by a facsimile of the President's signature. There was a card inside also with a handwritten note from the President which said, 'I hope you like these, Jack. I am assured they work! I thought they might be a reminder of something we still do quite well (perhaps too well?), followed by a scrawled signature just saying 'Brad', his first name. And, under the card, there was a properly signed and nicely framed studio photo of him. What a lovely present, I thought to myself, putting them away quickly in their box before one of the stewardesses saw them and had a heart attack.

And that was pretty much the end of my involvement in the case, except that, when I got back to the office, I showed the revolvers to Sir M who said, 'What do you intend to do with them, Jack? Kill more people?' I winced at his words and replied, 'I sincerely hope not, Sir.' I also showed them to the team and said I couldn't keep them at home as my wife would ask too many questions, which made them laugh. I continued that I'd like to donate them to the team and left them in Alan's capable hands to deal with as he wished, finding out later that he'd put them in our Black Museum and discreetly turned the pistols around so that my name wasn't visible. I kept the card in my safe and put the signed photo on the wall of my office, which elicited many admiring comments from visitors.

I visited Petrov a few more times, making sure he was happy, and followed his revelations with interest. He had certainly fallen on his feet, living in a Home Counties village and playing the part of village eccentric with gusto. He had also had plastic surgery done, altering the lines of his face subtly, and I hoped that would be enough to keep his old friends away.

The end

PS I obviously can't remember every word of every conversation that I had pertaining to the affair but I think I've managed to convey the gist of them.

PPS As you should know by now, I write these memoirs purely for my own benefit so that I have a written record of the important cases I have worked on and possibly for future generations of MI5 officers to learn something from. So, after several months of typing in every spare moment I had, I showed this manuscript to Sir M as I knew I had a duty to and asked him to bury it as deeply as possible in Records as he could and he promised to do so. He did, however, get back to me a few weeks later to say that he'd enjoyed reading it which was high praise indeed coming from him.

ABOUT THE AUTHOR

After graduating from university, Richard Sloane roamed the world for twenty years as a peripatetic English teacher with a couple of years back in England to do more studying. After that he returned to the city of his birth, Cambridge, to teach again for the next twenty years. However, he was then forced to retire due to medical reasons and since that time he has been writing fiction. He has written for all different age groups and this is his 18th published book.